The Most Dangerous Game

The Most Dangerous Game

And Other Stories of Menace and Adventure

by Jack London, Richard Connell, Ernest Hemingway, and More

STONEWELL PRESS

ISBN 978-1-62730-128-2

Published by Stonewell Press, Salt Lake City, Utah.

www.stonewellpress.com
editor@stonewellpress.com

Contents

The Most Dangerous Game 1
Captain Rogers 23
To Build a Fire 34
Leiningen versus the Ants 51
Sredni Vashtar 74
The Killers 79
An Occurrence at Owl Creek Bridge 89
The Country of the Blind 99

The Most Dangerous Game

Richard Connell

"Off there to the right—somewhere—is a large island," said Whitney." It's rather a mystery—"

"What island is it?" Rainsford asked.

"The old charts call it 'Ship-Trap Island,'" Whitney replied. "A suggestive name, isn't it? Sailors have a curious dread of the place. I don't know why. Some superstition—"

"Can't see it," remarked Rainsford, trying to peer through the dank tropical night that was palpable as it pressed its thick warm blackness in upon the yacht.

"You've good eyes," said Whitney, with a laugh, "and I've seen you pick off a moose moving in the brown fall bush at four hundred yards, but even you can't see four miles or so through a moonless Caribbean night."

"Nor four yards," admitted Rainsford. "Ugh! It's like moist black velvet."

"It will be light enough in Rio," promised Whitney. "We should make it in a few days. I hope the jaguar guns have come from Purdey's. We should have some good hunting up the Amazon. Great sport, hunting."

"The best sport in the world," agreed Rainsford.

"For the hunter," amended Whitney. "Not for the jaguar."

"Don't talk rot, Whitney," said Rainsford. "You're a big-game hunter, not a philosopher. Who cares how a jaguar feels?"

"Perhaps the jaguar does," observed Whitney.

"Bah! They've no understanding."

"Even so, I rather think they understand one thing—fear. The fear of pain and the fear of death."

"Nonsense," laughed Rainsford. "This hot weather is making you soft, Whitney. Be a realist. The world is made up of two classes—the hunters and the huntees. Luckily, you and I are hunters. Do you think we've passed that island yet?"

"I can't tell in the dark. I hope so."

"Why?" asked Rainsford.

"The place has a reputation—a bad one."

"Cannibals?" suggested Rainsford.

"Hardly. Even cannibals wouldn't live in such a God-forsaken place. But it's gotten into sailor lore, somehow. Didn't you notice that the crew's nerves seemed a bit jumpy today?"

"They were a bit strange, now you mention it. Even Captain Nielsen—"

"Yes, even that tough-minded old Swede, who'd go up to the devil himself and ask him for a light. Those fishy blue eyes held a look I never saw there before. All I could get out of him was 'This place has an evil name among seafaring men, sir.' Then he said to me, very gravely, 'Don't you feel anything?'—as if the air about us was actually poisonous. Now, you mustn't laugh when I tell you this—I did feel something like a sudden chill.

"There was no breeze. The sea was as flat as a plate-glass window. We were drawing near the island then. What I felt was a—a mental chill; a sort of sudden dread."

"Pure imagination," said Rainsford.

"One superstitious sailor can taint the whole ship's company with his fear."

"Maybe. But sometimes I think sailors have an extra sense that tells them when they are in danger. Sometimes I think evil is a tangible thing—with wave lengths, just as sound and light have. An evil place can, so to speak, broadcast vibrations of evil. Anyhow, I'm glad we're getting out of this zone. Well, I think I'll turn in now, Rainsford."

"I'm not sleepy," said Rainsford. "I'm going to smoke another pipe up on the afterdeck."

"Good night, then, Rainsford. See you at breakfast."

"Right. Good night, Whitney."

There was no sound in the night as Rainsford sat there but the muffled throb of the engine that drove the yacht swiftly through the darkness, and the swish and ripple of the wash of the propeller.

Rainsford, reclining in a steamer chair, indolently puffed on his favorite brier. The sensuous drowsiness of the night was on him. "It's so dark," he thought, "that I could sleep without closing my eyes; the night would be my eyelids—"

An abrupt sound startled him. Off to the right he heard it, and his ears, expert in such matters, could not be mistaken. Again he heard the sound, and again. Somewhere, off in the blackness, someone had fired a gun three times.

Rainsford sprang up and moved quickly to the rail, mystified. He strained his eyes in the direction from which the reports had come, but it was like trying to see through a blanket. He leaped upon the rail and balanced himself there, to get greater elevation; his pipe, striking a rope, was knocked from his mouth. He lunged for it; a short, hoarse cry came from his lips as he realized he had reached too far and had lost his balance. The cry was pinched off short as the blood-warm waters of the Caribbean Sea closed over his head.

He struggled up to the surface and tried to cry out, but the wash from the speeding yacht slapped him in the face and the salt water in his open mouth made him gag and strangle. Desperately he struck out with strong strokes after the receding lights of the yacht, but he stopped before he had swum fifty feet. A certain coolheadedness had come to him; it was not the first time he had been in a tight place. There was a chance that his cries could be heard by someone aboard the yacht, but that chance was slender and grew more slender as the yacht raced on. He wrestled himself out of his clothes and shouted with all his power. The lights of the yacht became faint and ever-vanishing fireflies; then they were blotted out entirely by the night.

Rainsford remembered the shots. They had come from the right, and doggedly he swam in that direction, swimming with slow, deliberate strokes, conserving his strength. For a seemingly endless time he fought the sea. He began to count his strokes; he could do possibly a hundred more and then—

Rainsford heard a sound. It came out of the darkness, a high screaming sound, the sound of an animal in an extremity of anguish and terror.

He did not recognize the animal that made the sound; he did not try to; with fresh vitality he swam toward the sound.

He heard it again; then it was cut short by another noise, crisp, staccato.

"Pistol shot," muttered Rainsford, swimming on.

Ten minutes of determined effort brought another sound to his ears—the most welcome he had ever heard—the muttering and growling of the sea breaking on a rocky shore. He was almost on the rocks before he saw them; on a night less calm he would have been shattered against them. With his remaining strength he dragged himself from the swirling waters. Jagged crags appeared to jut up into the opaqueness; he forced himself upward, hand over hand. Gasping, his hands raw, he reached a flat place at the top. Dense jungle came down to the very edge of the cliffs. What perils that tangle of trees and underbrush might hold for him did not concern Rainsford just then. All he knew was that he was safe from his enemy, the sea, and that utter weariness was on him. He flung himself down at the jungle edge and tumbled headlong into the deepest sleep of his life.

When he opened his eyes he knew from the position of the sun that it was late in the afternoon. Sleep had given him new vigor; a sharp hunger was picking at him. He looked about him, almost cheerfully.

"Where there are pistol shots, there are men. Where there are men, there is food," he thought. But what kind of men, he wondered, in so forbidding a place? An unbroken front of snarled and ragged jungle fringed the shore.

He saw no sign of a trail through the closely knit web of weeds and trees; it was easier to go along the shore, and Rainsford floundered along by the water. Not far from where he landed, he stopped.

Some wounded thing—by the evidence, a large animal—had thrashed about in the underbrush; the jungle weeds were crushed down and the moss was lacerated; one patch of weeds was stained crimson. A small, glittering object not far away caught Rainsford's eye and he picked it up. It was an empty cartridge.

"A twenty-two," he remarked. "That's odd. It must have been a fairly large animal too. The hunter had his nerve with him to tackle it with a light gun. It's clear that the brute put up a fight. I suppose the first three shots I heard were when the hunter flushed his quarry and wounded it. The last shot was when he trailed it here and finished it."

He examined the ground closely and found what he had hoped to find—the print of hunting boots. They pointed along the cliff in the direction he had been going. Eagerly he hurried along, now slipping on a rotten log or a loose stone, but making headway; night was beginning to settle down on the island.

Bleak darkness was blacking out the sea and jungle when Rainsford sighted the lights. He came upon them as he turned a crook in the coast line; and his first thought was that be had come upon a village, for there were many lights. But as he forged along he saw to his great astonishment that all the lights were in one enormous building—a lofty structure with pointed towers plunging upward into the gloom. His eyes made out the shadowy outlines of a palatial chateau; it was set on a high bluff, and on three sides of it cliffs dived down to where the sea licked greedy lips in the shadows.

"Mirage," thought Rainsford. But it was no mirage, he found, when he opened the tall spiked iron gate. The stone steps were real enough; the massive door with a leering gargoyle for a knocker was real enough; yet above it all hung an air of unreality.

He lifted the knocker, and it creaked up stiffly, as if it had never before been used. He let it fall, and it startled him with its booming loudness. He thought he heard steps within; the door remained closed. Again Rainsford lifted the heavy knocker, and let it fall. The door opened then—opened as suddenly as if it were on a spring—and Rainsford stood blinking in the river of glaring gold light that poured out. The first thing Rainsford's eyes discerned was the largest man Rainsford had ever seen—a gigantic creature, solidly made and black bearded to the waist. In his hand the man held a long-barreled revolver, and he was pointing it straight at Rainsford's heart.

Out of the snarl of beard two small eyes regarded Rainsford.

"Don't be alarmed," said Rainsford, with a smile which he hoped was disarming. "I'm no robber. I fell off a yacht. My name is Sanger Rainsford of New York City."

The menacing look in the eyes did not change. The revolver pointing as rigidly as if the giant were a statue. He gave no sign that he understood Rainsford's words, or that he had even heard them. He was dressed in uniform—a black uniform trimmed with gray astrakhan.

"I'm Sanger Rainsford of New York," Rainsford began again. "I fell off a yacht. I am hungry."

The man's only answer was to raise with his thumb the hammer of his revolver. Then Rainsford saw the man's free hand go to his forehead in a military salute, and he saw him click his heels together and stand at attention. Another man was coming down the broad marble steps, an erect, slender man in evening clothes. He advanced to Rainsford and held out his hand.

In a cultivated voice marked by a slight accent that gave it added precision and deliberateness, he said, "It is a very great pleasure and honor to welcome Mr. Sanger Rainsford, the celebrated hunter, to my home."

Automatically Rainsford shook the man's hand.

"I've read your book about hunting snow leopards in Tibet, you see," explained the man. "I am General Zaroff."

Rainsford's first impression was that the man was singularly handsome; his second was that there was an original, almost bizarre quality about the general's face. He was a tall man past middle age, for his hair was a vivid white; but his thick eyebrows and pointed military mustache were as black as the night from which Rainsford had come. His eyes, too, were black and very bright. He had high cheekbones, a sharpcut nose, a spare, dark face—the face of a man used to giving orders, the face of an aristocrat. Turning to the giant in uniform, the general made a sign. The giant put away his pistol, saluted, withdrew.

"Ivan is an incredibly strong fellow," remarked the general, "but he has the misfortune to be deaf and dumb. A simple fellow, but, I'm afraid, like all his race, a bit of a savage."

"Is he Russian?"

"He is a Cossack," said the general, and his smile showed red lips and pointed teeth. "So am I."

"Come," he said, "we shouldn't be chatting here. We can talk later. Now you want clothes, food, rest. You shall have them. This is a most-restful spot."

Ivan had reappeared, and the general spoke to him with lips that moved but gave forth no sound.

"Follow Ivan, if you please, Mr. Rainsford," said the general.

"I was about to have my dinner when you came. I'll wait for you. You'll find that my clothes will fit you, I think."

It was to a huge, beam-ceilinged bedroom with a canopied bed big enough for six men that Rainsford followed the silent giant. Ivan laid out an evening suit, and Rainsford, as he put it on, noticed that it came from a London tailor who ordinarily cut and sewed for none below the rank of duke.

The dining room to which Ivan conducted him was in many ways remarkable. There was a medieval magnificence about it; it suggested a baronial hall of feudal times with its oaken panels, its high ceiling, its vast refectory tables where twoscore men could sit down to eat. About the hall were mounted heads of many animals—lions, tigers, elephants, moose, bears; larger or more perfect specimens Rainsford had never seen. At the great table the general was sitting, alone.

"You'll have a cocktail, Mr. Rainsford," he suggested. The cocktail was surpassingly good; and, Rainsford noted, the table appointments were of the finest—the linen, the crystal, the silver, the china.

They were eating *borsch,* the rich, red soup with whipped cream so dear to Russian palates. Half apologetically General Zaroff said, "We do our best to preserve the amenities of civilization here. Please forgive any lapses. We are well off the beaten track, you know. Do you think the champagne has suffered from its long ocean trip?"

"Not in the least," declared Rainsford. He was finding the general a most thoughtful and affable host, a true cosmopolite. But there was one small trait of the general's that made Rainsford uncomfortable. Whenever he looked up from his plate he found the general studying him, appraising him narrowly.

"Perhaps," said General Zaroff, "you were surprised that I recognized your name. You see, I read all books on hunting published in English, French, and Russian. I have but one passion in my life, Mr. Rainsford, and it is the hunt."

"You have some wonderful heads here," said Rainsford as he ate a particularly well-cooked *filet mignon.* "That Cape buffalo is the largest I ever saw."

"Oh, that fellow. Yes, he was a monster."

"Did he charge you?"

"Hurled me against a tree," said the general. "Fractured my skull. But I got the brute."

"I've always thought," said Rainsford, "that the Cape buffalo is the most dangerous of all big game."

For a moment the general did not reply; he was smiling his curious red-lipped smile. Then he said slowly, "No. You are wrong, sir. The Cape buffalo is not the most dangerous big game." He sipped his wine. "Here in my preserve on this island," he said in the same slow tone, "I hunt more dangerous game."

Rainsford expressed his surprise. "Is there big game on this island?"

The general nodded. "The biggest."

"Really?"

"Oh, it isn't here naturally, of course. I have to stock the island."

"What have you imported, general?" Rainsford asked. "Tigers?"

The general smiled. "No," he said. "Hunting tigers ceased to interest me some years ago. I exhausted their possibilities, you see. No thrill left in tigers, no real danger. I live for danger, Mr. Rainsford."

The general took from his pocket a gold cigarette case and offered his guest a long black cigarette with a silver tip; it was perfumed and gave off a smell like incense.

"We will have some capital hunting, you and I," said the general. "I shall be most glad to have your society."

"But what game—" began Rainsford.

"I'll tell you," said the general. "You will be amused, I know. I think I may say, in all modesty, that I have done a rare thing. I have invented a new sensation. May I pour you another glass of port?"

"Thank you, general."

The general filled both glasses, and said, "God makes some men poets. Some He makes kings, some beggars. Me He made a hunter. My hand was made for the trigger, my father said. He was a very rich man with a quarter of a million acres in the Crimea, and he was an ardent sportsman. When I was only five years old he gave me a little gun, specially made in Moscow for me, to shoot sparrows with. When I shot some of his prize turkeys with it, he did not punish me; he complimented me on my marksmanship. I killed my first bear in the Caucasus when I was ten. My whole life has been one prolonged hunt. I went into the army—it was expected of noblemen's sons—and for a time commanded a division of Cossack cavalry, but my real interest was always the hunt. I have hunted every kind of game in every land. It would be impossible for me to tell you how many animals I have killed."

The general puffed at his cigarette.

"After the debacle in Russia I left the country, for it was imprudent for an officer of the Czar to stay there. Many noble Russians lost everything. I, luckily, had invested heavily in American securities, so I shall never have to open a tearoom in Monte Carlo or drive a taxi in Paris. Naturally, I continued to hunt—grizzlies in your Rockies, crocodiles in the Ganges, rhinoceroses in East Africa. It was in Africa that the Cape buffalo hit me and laid me up for six months. As soon as I recovered I started for the Amazon to hunt jaguars, for I had heard they were unusually cunning. They weren't." The Cossack sighed. "They were no match at all for a hunter with his wits about him, and a high-powered rifle. I was bitterly disappointed. I was lying in my tent with a splitting headache one night when a terrible thought pushed its way into my mind. Hunting was beginning to bore me! And hunting, remember, had been my life. I have heard that in America businessmen often go to pieces when they give up the business that has been their life."

"Yes, that's so," said Rainsford.

The general smiled. "I had no wish to go to pieces," he said. "I must do something. Now, mine is an analytical mind, Mr. Rainsford. Doubtless that is why I enjoy the problems of the chase."

"No doubt, General Zaroff."

"So," continued the general, "I asked myself why the hunt no longer fascinated me. You are much younger than I am, Mr. Rainsford, and have not hunted as much, but you perhaps can guess the answer."

"What was it?"

"Simply this: hunting had ceased to be what you call 'a sporting proposition.' It had become too easy. I always got my quarry. Always. There is no greater bore than perfection."

The general lit a fresh cigarette.

"No animal had a chance with me any more. That is no boast; it is a mathematical certainty. The animal had nothing but his legs and his instinct. Instinct is no match for reason. When I thought of this it was a tragic moment for me, I can tell you."

Rainsford leaned across the table, absorbed in what his host was saying.

"It came to me as an inspiration what I must do," the general went on.

"And that was?"

The general smiled the quiet smile of one who has faced an obstacle and surmounted it with success. "I had to invent a new animal to hunt," he said.

"A new animal? You're joking."

"Not at all," said the general. "I never joke about hunting. I needed a new animal. I found one. So I bought this island, built this house, and here I do my hunting. The island is perfect for my purposes—there are jungles with a maze of traits in them, hills, swamps—"

"But the animal, General Zaroff?"

"Oh," said the general, "it supplies me with the most exciting hunting in the world. No other hunting compares with it for an instant. Every day I hunt, and I never grow bored now, for I have a quarry with which I can match my wits."

Rainsford's bewilderment showed in his face.

"I wanted the ideal animal to hunt," explained the general. "So I said, 'What are the attributes of an ideal quarry?' And the answer was, of course, 'It must have courage, cunning, and, above all, it must be able to reason.'"

"But no animal can reason," objected Rainsford.

"My dear fellow," said the general, "there is one that can."

"But you can't mean—" gasped Rainsford.

"And why not?"

"I can't believe you are serious, General Zaroff. This is a grisly joke."

"Why should I not be serious? I am speaking of hunting."

"Hunting? Great Guns, General Zaroff, what you speak of is murder."

The general laughed with entire good nature. He regarded

Rainsford quizzically. "I refuse to believe that so modern and civilized a young man as you seem to be harbors romantic ideas about the value of human life. Surely your experiences in the war—"

"Did not make me condone cold-blooded murder," finished Rainsford stiffly.

Laughter shook the general. "How extraordinarily droll you are!" he said. "One does not expect nowadays to find a young man of the educated class, even in America, with such a naive, and, if I may say so, mid-Victorian point of view. It's like finding a snuffbox in a limousine. Ah, well, doubtless you had Puritan ancestors. So many Americans appear to have had. I'll wager you'll forget your notions when you go hunting with me. You've a genuine new thrill in store for you, Mr. Rainsford."

"Thank you, I'm a hunter, not a murderer."

"Dear me," said the general, quite unruffled, "again that unpleasant word. But I think I can show you that your scruples are quite ill founded."

"Yes?"

"Life is for the strong, to be lived by the strong, and, if needs be, taken by the strong. The weak of the world were put here to give the strong pleasure. I am strong. Why should I not use my gift? If I wish to hunt, why should I not? I hunt the scum of the earth: sailors from tramp ships—lassars, blacks, Chinese, whites, mongrels—a thoroughbred horse or hound is worth more than a score of them."

"But they are men," said Rainsford hotly.

"Precisely," said the general. "That is why I use them. It gives me pleasure. They can reason, after a fashion. So they are dangerous."

"But where do you get them?"

The general's left eyelid fluttered down in a wink. "This island is called Ship Trap," he answered. "Sometimes an angry god of the high seas sends them to me. Sometimes, when Providence is not so kind, I help Providence a bit. Come to the window with me."

Rainsford went to the window and looked out toward the sea.

"Watch! Out there!" exclaimed the general, pointing into the night. Rainsford's eyes saw only blackness, and then, as the general pressed a button, far out to sea Rainsford saw the flash of lights.

The general chuckled. "They indicate a channel," he said, "where there's none; giant rocks with razor edges crouch like a sea monster with wide-open jaws. They can crush a ship as easily as I crush this nut." He dropped a walnut on the hardwood floor and brought his heel grinding down on it. "Oh, yes," he said, casually, as if in answer to a question, "I have electricity. We try to be civilized here."

"Civilized? And you shoot down men?"

A trace of anger was in the general's black eyes, but it was there for but a second; and he said, in his most pleasant manner, "Dear me, what a righteous young man you are! I assure you I do not do the thing you suggest. That would be barbarous. I treat these visitors with every consideration. They get plenty of good food and exercise. They get into splendid physical condition. You shall see for yourself tomorrow."

"What do you mean?"

"We'll visit my training school," smiled the general. "It's in the cellar. I have about a dozen pupils down there now. They're from the Spanish bark *San Lucar* that had the bad luck to go on the rocks out there. A very inferior lot, I regret to say. Poor specimens and more accustomed to the deck than to the jungle." He raised his hand, and Ivan, who served as waiter, brought thick Turkish coffee. Rainsford, with an effort, held his tongue in check.

"It's a game, you see," pursued the general blandly. "I suggest to one of them that we go hunting. I give him a supply of food and an excellent hunting knife. I give him three hours' start. I am to follow, armed only with a pistol of the smallest caliber and range. If my quarry eludes me for three whole days, he wins the game. If I find him"—the general smiled—"he loses."

"Suppose he refuses to be hunted?"

"Oh," said the general, "I give him his option, of course. He need not play that game if he doesn't wish to. If he does not wish to hunt, I turn him over to Ivan. Ivan once had the honor of serving as official knouter to the Great White Czar, and he has his own ideas of sport. Invariably, Mr. Rainsford, invariably they choose the hunt."

"And if they win?"

The smile on the general's face widened. "To date I have not lost," he said. Then he added, hastily: "I don't wish you to think me a braggart, Mr. Rainsford. Many of them afford only the most elementary sort of problem. Occasionally I strike a tartar. One almost did win. I eventually had to use the dogs."

"The dogs?"

"This way, please. I'll show you."

The general steered Rainsford to a window. The lights from the windows sent a flickering illumination that made grotesque patterns on the courtyard below, and Rainsford could see moving about there a dozen or so huge black shapes; as they turned toward him, their eyes glittered greenly.

"A rather good lot, I think," observed the general. "They are let out at seven every night. If anyone should try to get into my house—or out of it—something extremely regrettable would occur to him." He hummed a snatch of song from the *Folies Bergere.*

"And now," said the general, "I want to show you my new collection of heads. Will you come with me to the library?"

"I hope," said Rainsford, "that you will excuse me tonight, General Zaroff. I'm really not feeling well."

"Ah, indeed?" the general inquired solicitously. "Well, I suppose that's only natural, after your long swim. You need a good, restful night's sleep. Tomorrow you'll feel like a new man, I'll wager. Then we'll hunt, eh? I've one rather promising prospect—" Rainsford was hurrying from the room.

"Sorry you can't go with me tonight," called the general. "I expect rather fair sport—a big, strong black. He looks resourceful—Well, good night, Mr. Rainsford; I hope you have a good night's rest."

The bed was good, and the pajamas of the softest silk, and he was tired in every fiber of his being, but nevertheless Rainsford could not quiet his brain with the opiate of sleep. He lay, eyes wide open. Once he thought he heard stealthy steps in the corridor outside his room. He sought to throw open the door; it would not open. He went to the window and looked out. His room was high up in one of the towers. The lights of the chateau were out now, and it was dark and silent; but there was a fragment of sallow moon, and by its wan light he could see, dimly, the courtyard. There, weaving in and out in the pattern of shadow, were black, noiseless forms; the hounds heard him at the window and looked up, expectantly, with their green eyes. Rainsford went back to the bed and lay down. By many methods he tried to put himself to sleep. He had achieved a doze when, just as morning began to come, he heard, far off in the jungle, the faint report of a pistol.

* * *

General Zaroff did not appear until luncheon. He was dressed faultlessly in the tweeds of a country squire. He was solicitous about the state of Rainsford's health.

"As for me," sighed the general, "I do not feel so well. I am worried, Mr. Rainsford. Last night I detected traces of my old complaint."

To Rainsford's questioning glance the general said, "Ennui. Boredom."

Then, taking a second helping of *crêpes Suzette,* the general explained: "The hunting was not good last night. The fellow lost his head. He made a straight trail that offered no problems at all. That's the trouble with these sailors; they have dull brains to begin with, and they do not know how to get about in the woods. They do excessively stupid and obvious things. It's most annoying. Will you have another glass of *Chablis,* Mr. Rainsford?"

"General," said Rainsford firmly, "I wish to leave this island at once."

The general raised his thickets of eyebrows; he seemed hurt. "But, my dear fellow," the general protested, "you've only just come. You've had no hunting—"

"I wish to go today," said Rainsford. He saw the dead black eyes of the general on him, studying him. General Zaroff's face suddenly brightened.

He filled Rainsford's glass with venerable *Chablis* from a dusty bottle.

"Tonight," said the general, "we will hunt—you and I."

Rainsford shook his head. "No, general," he said. "I will not hunt."

The general shrugged his shoulders and delicately ate a hothouse grape. "As you wish, my friend," he said. "The choice rests entirely with you. But may I not venture to suggest that you will find my idea of sport more diverting than Ivan's?"

He nodded toward the corner to where the giant stood, scowling, his thick arms crossed on his hogshead of chest.

"You don't mean—" cried Rainsford.

"My dear fellow," said the general, "have I not told you I always mean what I say about hunting? This is really an inspiration. I drink to a foeman worthy of my steel—at last." The general raised his glass, but Rainsford sat staring at him.

"You'll find this game worth playing," the general said enthusiastically." Your brain against mine. Your woodcraft against mine. Your strength and stamina against mine. Outdoor chess! And the stake is not without value, eh?"

"And if I win—" began Rainsford huskily.

"I'll cheerfully acknowledge myself defeated if I do not find you by midnight of the third day," said General Zaroff. "My sloop will place you on the mainland near a town." The general read what Rainsford was thinking.

"Oh, you can trust me," said the Cossack. "I will give you my word as a gentleman and a sportsman. Of course you, in turn, must agree to say nothing of your visit here."

"I'll agree to nothing of the kind," said Rainsford.

"Oh," said the general, "in that case—But why discuss that now? Three days hence we can discuss it over a bottle of *Veuve Cliquot,* unless—"

The general sipped his wine.

Then a businesslike air animated him. "Ivan," he said to Rainsford, "will supply you with hunting clothes, food, a knife. I suggest you wear moccasins; they leave a poorer trail. I suggest, too, that you avoid the big swamp in the southeast corner of the island. We call it Death Swamp. There's quicksand there. One foolish fellow tried it. The deplorable part of it was that Lazarus followed him. You can imagine my feelings, Mr. Rainsford. I loved Lazarus; he was the finest hound in my pack. Well, I must beg you to excuse me now. I always take a siesta after lunch. You'll hardly have time for a nap, I fear. You'll want to start, no doubt. I shall not follow till dusk. Hunting at night is so much more exciting than by day, don't you think? Au revoir, Mr.

Rainsford, au revoir." General Zaroff, with a deep, courtly bow, strolled from the room.

From another door came Ivan. Under one arm he carried khaki hunting clothes, a haversack of food, a leather sheath containing a long-bladed hunting knife; his right hand rested on a cocked revolver thrust in the crimson sash about his waist.

* * *

Rainsford had fought his way through the bush for two hours. "I must keep my nerve. I must keep my nerve," he said through tight teeth.

He had not been entirely clearheaded when the chateau gates snapped shut behind him. His whole idea at first was to put distance between himself and General Zaroff; and, to this end, he had plunged along, spurred on by the sharp powers of something very like panic. Now he had got a grip on himself, had stopped, and was taking stock of himself and the situation. He saw that straight flight was futile; inevitably it would bring him face to face with the sea. He was in a picture with a frame of water, and his operations, clearly, must take place within that frame.

"I'll give him a trail to follow," muttered Rainsford, and he struck off from the rude path he had been following into the trackless wilderness. He executed a series of intricate loops; he doubled on his trail again and again, recalling all the lore of the fox hunt, and all the dodges of the fox. Night found him leg-weary, with hands and face lashed by the branches, on a thickly wooded ridge. He knew it would be insane to blunder on through the dark, even if he had the strength. His need for rest was imperative and he thought, "I have played the fox, now I must play the cat of the fable." A big tree with a thick trunk and outspread branches was near by, and, taking care to leave not the slightest mark, he climbed up into the crotch, and, stretching out on one of the broad limbs, after a fashion, rested. Rest brought him new confidence and almost a feeling of security. Even so zealous a hunter as General Zaroff could not trace him there, he told himself; only the devil himself could follow that complicated trail through the jungle after dark. But perhaps the general was a devil—

An apprehensive night crawled slowly by like a wounded snake and sleep did not visit Rainsford, although the silence of a dead world was on the jungle. Toward morning when a dingy gray was varnishing the sky, the cry of some startled bird focused Rainsford's attention in that direction. Something was coming through the bush, coming slowly, carefully, coming by the same winding way Rainsford had come. He flattened himself down on the limb and, through a screen of leaves almost as thick as tapestry, he watched. . . . That which was approaching was a man.

It was General Zaroff. He made his way along with his eyes fixed in utmost concentration on the ground before him. He paused, almost beneath the tree, dropped to his knees and studied the ground. Rainsford's impulse was to hurl himself down like a panther, but he saw that the general's right hand held something metallic—a small automatic pistol.

The hunter shook his head several times, as if he were puzzled. Then he straightened up and took from his case one of his black cigarettes; its pungent incenselike smoke floated up to Rainsford's nostrils.

Rainsford held his breath. The general's eyes had left the ground and were traveling inch by inch up the tree. Rainsford froze there, every muscle tensed for a spring. But the sharp eyes of the hunter stopped before they reached the limb where Rainsford lay; a smile spread over his brown face. Very deliberately he blew a smoke ring into the air; then he turned his back on the tree and walked carelessly away, back along the trail he had come. The swish of the underbrush against his hunting boots grew fainter and fainter.

The pent-up air burst hotly from Rainsford's lungs. His first thought made him feel sick and numb. The general could follow a trail through the woods at night; he could follow an extremely difficult trail; he must have uncanny powers; only by the merest chance had the Cossack failed to see his quarry.

Rainsford's second thought was even more terrible. It sent a shudder of cold horror through his whole being. Why had the general smiled? Why had he turned back?

Rainsford did not want to believe what his reason told him was true, but the truth was as evident as the sun that had by now pushed through the morning mists. The general was playing with him! The general was saving him for another day's sport! The Cossack was the cat; he was the mouse. Then it was that Rainsford knew the full meaning of terror.

"I will not lose my nerve. I will not."

He slid down from the tree, and struck off again into the woods. His face was set and he forced the machinery of his mind to function. Three hundred yards from his hiding place he stopped where a huge dead tree leaned precariously on a smaller, living one. Throwing off his sack of food, Rainsford took his knife from its sheath and began to work with all his energy.

The job was finished at last, and he threw himself down behind a fallen log a hundred feet away. He did not have to wait long. The cat was coming again to play with the mouse.

Following the trail with the sureness of a bloodhound came General Zaroff. Nothing escaped those searching black eyes, no crushed blade of grass, no bent twig, no mark, no matter how faint, in the moss. So intent was the Cossack on his stalking that he was upon the thing Rainsford had made before he saw it. His foot touched the protruding bough that was the trigger. Even as he touched it, the general sensed his danger and leaped back with the agility of an ape. But he was not quite quick enough; the dead tree, delicately adjusted to rest on the cut living one, crashed down and struck the general a glancing blow on the shoulder as it fell; but for his alertness, he must have been smashed beneath it. He staggered, but he did not fall; nor did he drop his revolver. He stood there, rubbing his injured shoulder, and Rainsford, with fear again gripping his heart, heard the general's mocking laugh ring through the jungle.

"Rainsford," called the general, "if you are within sound of my voice, as I suppose you are, let me congratulate you. Not many men know how to make a Malay mancatcher. Luckily for me I, too, have hunted in Malacca. You are proving interesting, Mr. Rainsford. I am going now to have my wound dressed; it's only a slight one. But I shall be back. I shall be back."

When the general, nursing his bruised shoulder, had gone, Rainsford took up his flight again. It was flight now, a desperate, hopeless flight, that carried him on for some hours. Dusk came, then darkness, and still he pressed on. The ground grew softer under his moccasins; the vegetation grew ranker, denser; insects bit him savagely.

Then, as he stepped forward, his foot sank into the ooze. He tried to wrench it back, but the muck sucked viciously at his foot as if it were a giant leech. With a violent effort, he tore his feet loose. He knew where he was now. Death Swamp and its quicksand.

His hands were tight closed as if his nerve were something tangible that someone in the darkness was trying to tear from his grip. The softness of the earth had given him an idea. He stepped back from the quicksand a dozen feet or so and, like some huge prehistoric beaver, he began to dig.

Rainsford had dug himself in in France when a second's delay meant death. That had been a placid pastime compared to his digging now. The pit grew deeper; when it was above his shoulders, he climbed out and from some hard saplings cut stakes and sharpened them to a fine point. These stakes he planted in the bottom of the pit with the points sticking up. With flying fingers he wove a rough carpet of weeds and branches and with it he covered the mouth of the pit. Then, wet with sweat and aching with tiredness, he crouched behind the stump of a lightning-charred tree.

He knew his pursuer was coming; he heard the padding sound of feet on the soft earth, and the night breeze brought him the perfume of the general's cigarette. It seemed to Rainsford that the general was coming with unusual swiftness; he was not feeling his way along, foot by foot. Rainsford, crouching there, could not see the general, nor could he see the pit. He lived a year in a minute. Then he felt an impulse to cry aloud with joy, for he heard the sharp crackle of the breaking branches as the cover of the pit gave way; he heard the sharp scream of pain as the pointed stakes found their mark. He leaped up from his place of concealment. Then he cowered back. Three feet from the pit a man was standing, with an electric torch in his hand.

"You've done well, Rainsford," the voice of the general called. "Your Burmese tiger pit has claimed one of my best dogs. Again you score. I think, Mr. Rainsford, I'll see what you can do against my whole pack. I'm going home for a rest now. Thank you for a most amusing evening."

At daybreak Rainsford, lying near the swamp, was awakened by a sound that made him know that he had new things to learn about fear. It was a distant sound, faint and wavering, but he knew it. It was the baying of a pack of hounds.

Rainsford knew he could do one of two things. He could stay where he was and wait. That was suicide. He could flee. That was postponing the inevitable. For a moment he stood there, thinking. An idea that held a wild chance came to him, and, tightening his belt, he headed away from the swamp.

The baying of the hounds drew nearer, then still nearer, nearer, ever nearer. On a ridge Rainsford climbed a tree. Down a watercourse, not a quarter of a mile away, he could see the bush moving. Straining his eyes, he saw the lean figure of General Zaroff; just ahead of him Rainsford made out another figure whose wide shoulders surged through the tall jungle weeds; it was the giant Ivan, and he seemed pulled forward by some unseen force; Rainsford knew that Ivan must be holding the pack in leash.

They would be on him any minute now. His mind worked frantically. He thought of a native trick he had learned in Uganda. He slid down the tree. He caught hold of a springy young sapling and to it he fastened his hunting knife, with the blade pointing down the trail; with a bit of wild grapevine he tied back the sapling. Then he ran for his life. The hounds raised their voices as they hit the fresh scent. Rainsford knew now how an animal at bay feels.

He had to stop to get his breath. The baying of the hounds stopped abruptly, and Rainsford's heart stopped too. They must have reached the knife.

He shinned excitedly up a tree and looked back. His pursuers had stopped. But the hope that was in Rainsford's brain when he climbed died, for he saw in the shallow valley that General Zaroff was still on his feet. But Ivan was not. The knife, driven by the recoil of the springing tree, had not wholly failed.

Rainsford had hardly tumbled to the ground when the pack took up the cry again.

"Nerve, nerve, nerve!" he panted, as he dashed along. A blue gap showed between the trees dead ahead. Ever nearer drew the hounds. Rainsford forced himself on toward that gap. He reached it. It was the shore of the sea. Across a cove he could see the gloomy gray stone of the chateau. Twenty feet below him the sea rumbled and hissed. Rainsford hesitated. He heard the hounds. Then he leaped far out into the sea. . . .

When the general and his pack reached the place by the sea, the Cossack stopped. For some minutes he stood regarding the blue-green expanse of water. He shrugged his shoulders. Then he sat down, took a drink of brandy from a silver flask, lit a cigarette, and hummed a bit from *Madame Butterfly*.

* * *

General Zaroff had an exceedingly good dinner in his great paneled dining hall that evening. With it he had a bottle of *Pol Roger* and half a bottle of *Chambertin*. Two slight annoyances kept him from perfect enjoyment. One was the thought that it would be difficult to replace Ivan; the other was that his quarry had escaped him; of course, the American hadn't played the game—so thought the general as he tasted his after-dinner liqueur. In his library he read, to soothe himself, from the works of Marcus Aurelius. At ten he went up to his bedroom. He was deliciously tired, he said to himself, as he locked himself in. There was a little moonlight, so, before turning on his light, he went to the window and looked down at the courtyard. He could see the great hounds, and he called, "Better luck another time," to them. Then he switched on the light.

A man, who had been hiding in the curtains of the bed, was standing there.

"Rainsford!" screamed the general. "How in God's name did you get here?"

"Swam," said Rainsford. "I found it quicker than walking through the jungle."

The general sucked in his breath and smiled. "I congratulate you," he said. "You have won the game."

Rainsford did not smile. "I am still a beast at bay," he said, in a low, hoarse voice. "Get ready, General Zaroff."

The general made one of his deepest bows. "I see," he said. "Splendid! One of us is to furnish a repast for the hounds. The other will sleep in this very excellent bed. On guard, Rainsford." . . .

He had never slept in a better bed, Rainsford decided.

Captain Rogers

W. W. Jacobs

A man came slowly over the old stone bridge, and averting his gaze from the dark river with its silent craft, looked with some satisfaction toward the feeble lights of the small town on the other side. He walked with the painful, forced step of one who has already trudged far. His worsted hose, where they were not darned, were in holes, and his coat and knee-breeches were rusty with much wear, but he straightened himself as he reached the end of the bridge and stepped out bravely to the taverns which stood in a row facing the quay.

He passed the "Queen Anne"—a mere beershop—without pausing, and after a glance apiece at the "Royal George" and the "Trusty Anchor," kept on his way to where the "Golden Key" hung out a gilded emblem. It was the best house in Riverstone, and patronized by the gentry, but he adjusted his faded coat, and with a swaggering air entered and walked boldly into the coffee-room.

The room was empty, but a bright fire afforded a pleasant change to the chill October air outside. He drew up a chair, and placing his feet on the fender, exposed his tattered soles to the blaze, as a waiter who had just seen him enter the room came and stood aggressively inside the door.

"Brandy and water," said the stranger; "hot."

"The coffee-room is for gentlemen staying in the house," said the waiter.

The stranger took his feet from the fender, and rising slowly, walked toward him. He was a short man and thin, but there was something so menacing in his attitude, and something so fearsome in his stony brown eyes, that the other, despite his disgust for ill-dressed people, moved back uneasily.

"Brandy and water, hot," repeated the stranger; "and plenty of it. D'ye hear?"

The man turned slowly to depart.

"Stop!" said the other, imperiously. "What's the name of the landlord here?"

"Mullet," said the fellow, sulkily.

"Send him to me," said the other, resuming his seat; "and hark you, my friend, more civility, or 'twill be the worse for you."

He stirred the log on the fire with his foot until a shower of sparks whirled up the chimney. The door opened, and the landlord, with the waiter behind him, entered the room, but he still gazed placidly at the glowing embers.

"What do you want?" demanded the landlord, in a deep voice.

The stranger turned a little wizened yellow face and grinned at him familiarly.

"Send that fat rascal of yours away," he said, slowly.

The landlord started at his voice and eyed him closely; then he signed to the man to withdraw, and closing the door behind him, stood silently watching his visitor.

"You didn't expect to see me, Rogers," said the latter.

"My name's Mullet," said the other, sternly. "What do you want?"

"Oh, Mullet?" said the other, in surprise. "I'm afraid I've made a mistake, then. I thought you were my old shipmate, Captain Rogers. It's a foolish mistake of mine, as I've no doubt Rogers was hanged years ago. You never had a brother named Rogers, did you?"

"I say again, what do you want?" demanded the other, advancing upon him.

"Since you're so good," said the other. "I want new clothes, food, and lodging of the best, and my pockets filled with money."

"You had better go and look for all those things, then," said Mullet. "You won't find them here."

"Ay!" said the other, rising. "Well, well—There was a hundred guineas on the head of my old shipmate Rogers some fifteen years ago. I'll see whether it has been earned yet."

"If I gave you a hundred guineas," said the innkeeper, repressing his passion by a mighty effort, "you would not be satisfied."

"Reads like a book," said the stranger, in tones of pretended delight. "What a man it is!"

He fell back as he spoke, and thrusting his hand into his pocket, drew forth a long pistol as the innkeeper, a man of huge frame, edged toward him.

"Keep your distance," he said, in a sharp, quick voice.

The innkeeper, in no wise disturbed at the pistol, turned away calmly, and ringing the bell, ordered some spirits. Then taking a chair, he motioned to the other to do the same, and they sat in silence until the staring waiter had left the room again. The stranger raised his glass.

"My old friend Captain Rogers," he said, solemnly, "and may he never get his deserts!"

"From what jail have you come?" inquired Mullet, sternly.

"'Pon my soul," said the other, "I have been in so many—looking for Captain Rogers—that I almost forget the last, but I have just tramped from London, two hundred and eighty odd miles, for the pleasure of seeing your damned ugly figure-head again; and now I've found it, I'm going to stay. Give me some money."

The innkeeper, without a word, drew a little gold and silver from his pocket, and placing it on the table, pushed it toward him.

"Enough to go on with," said the other, pocketing it; "in future it is halves. D'ye hear me? Halves! And I'll stay here and see I get it."

He sat back in his chair, and meeting the other's hatred with a gaze as steady as his own, replaced his pistol.

"A nice snug harbor after our many voyages," he continued. "Shipmates we were, shipmates we'll be; while Nick Gunn is alive you shall never want for company. Lord! Do you remember the Dutch brig, and the fat frightened mate?"

"I have forgotten it," said the other, still eyeing him steadfastly. "I have forgotten many things. For fifteen years I have lived a decent, honest life. Pray God for your own sinful soul, that the devil in me does not wake again."

"Fifteen years is a long nap," said Gunn, carelessly; "what a godsend it'll be for you to have me by you to remind you of old times! Why, you're looking smug, man; the honest innkeeper to the life! Gad! who's the girl?"

He rose and made a clumsy bow as a girl of eighteen, after a moment's hesitation at the door, crossed over to the innkeeper.

"I'm busy, my dear," said the latter, somewhat sternly.

"Our business," said Gunn, with another bow, "is finished. Is this your daughter, Rog—Mullet?"

"My stepdaughter," was the reply.

Gunn placed a hand, which lacked two fingers, on his breast, and bowed again.

"One of your father's oldest friends," he said smoothly; "and fallen on evil days; I'm sure your gentle heart will be pleased to hear that your good father has requested me—for a time—to make his house my home."

"Any friend of my father's is welcome to me, sir," said the girl, coldly. She looked from the innkeeper to his odd-looking guest, and conscious of something strained in the air, gave him a little bow and quitted the room.

"You insist upon staying, then?" said Mullet, after a pause.

"More than ever," replied Gunn, with a leer toward the door. "Why, you don't think I'm *afraid,* Captain? You should know me better than that."

"Life is sweet," said the other.

"Ay," assented Gunn, "so sweet that you will share things with me to keep it."

"No," said the other, with great calm. "I am man enough to have a better reason."

"No psalm singing," said Gunn, coarsely. "And look cheerful, you old buccaneer. Look as a man should look who has just met an old friend never to lose him again."

He eyed his man expectantly and put his hand to his pocket again, but the innkeeper's face was troubled, and he gazed stolidly at the fire.

"See what fifteen years' honest, decent life does for us," grinned the intruder.

The other made no reply, but rising slowly, walked to the door without a word.

"Landlord," cried Gunn, bringing his maimed hand sharply down on the table.

The innkeeper turned and regarded him.

"Send me in some supper," said Gunn; "the best you have, and plenty of it, and have a room prepared. The best."

The door closed silently, and was opened a little later by the dubious George coming in to set a bountiful repast. Gunn, after cursing him for his slowness and awkwardness, drew his chair to the table and made the meal of one seldom able to satisfy his hunger. He finished at last, and after sitting for some time smoking, with his legs sprawled on the fender, rang for a candle and demanded to be shown to his room.

His proceedings when he entered it were but a poor compliment to his host. Not until he had poked and pried into every corner did he close the door. Then, not content with locking it, he tilted a chair beneath the handle, and placing his pistol beneath his pillow, fell fast asleep.

Despite his fatigue he was early astir next morning. Breakfast was laid for him in the coffee-room, and his brow darkened. He walked into the hall, and after trying various doors entered a small sitting-room, where his host and daughter sat at breakfast, and with an easy assurance drew a chair to the table. The innkeeper helped him without a word, but the girl's hand shook under his gaze as she passed him some coffee.

"As soft a bed as ever I slept in," he remarked.

"I hope that you slept well," said the girl, civilly.

"Like a child," said Gunn, gravely; "an easy conscience. Eh, Mullet?"

The innkeeper nodded and went on eating. The other, after another remark or two, followed his example, glancing occasionally with warm approval at the beauty of the girl who sat at the head of the table.

"A sweet girl," he remarked, as she withdrew at the end of the meal; "and no mother, I presume?"

"No mother," repeated the other.

Gunn sighed and shook his head.

"A sad case, truly," he murmured. "No mother and such a guardian. Poor soul, if she but knew! Well, we must find her a husband."

He looked down as he spoke, and catching sight of his rusty clothes and broken shoes, clapped his hand to his pocket; and with a glance at his host, sallied out to renew his wardrobe. The innkeeper, with an inscrutable face, watched him down the quay, then with bent head he returned to the house and fell to work on his accounts.

In this work Gunn, returning an hour later, clad from head to foot in new apparel, offered to assist him. Mullet hesitated, but made no demur; neither did he join in the ecstasies which his new partner displayed at the sight of the profits. Gunn put some more gold into his new pockets, and throwing himself back in a chair, called loudly to George to bring him some drink.

In less than a month the intruder was the virtual master of the "Golden Key." Resistance on the part of the legitimate owner became more and more feeble, the slightest objection on his part drawing from the truculent Gunn dark allusions to his past and threats against his future, which for the sake of his daughter he could not ignore. His health began to fail, and Joan watched with perplexed terror the growth of a situation which was in a fair way of becoming unbearable.

The arrogance of Gunn knew no bounds. The maids learned to tremble at his polite grin, or his worse freedom, and the men shrank appalled from his profane wrath. George, after ten years' service, was brutally dismissed, and refusing to accept dismissal from his hands, appealed to his master. The innkeeper confirmed it, and with lack-lustre eyes fenced feebly when his daughter, regardless of Gunn's presence, indignantly appealed to him.

"The man was rude to my friend, my dear," he said dispiritedly.

"If he was rude, it was because Mr. Gunn deserved it," said Joan, hotly.

Gunn laughed uproariously.

"Gad, my dear, I like you!" he cried, slapping his leg. "You're a girl of spirit. Now I will make you a fair offer. If you ask for George to stay, stay he shall, as a favor to your sweet self."

The girl trembled.

"Who is master here?" she demanded, turning a full eye on her father.

Mullet laughed uneasily.

"This is business," he said, trying to speak lightly, "and women can't understand it. Gunn is—is valuable to me, and George must go."

"Unless you plead for him, sweet one?" said Gunn.

The girl looked at her father again, but he turned his head away and tapped on the floor with his foot. Then in perplexity, akin to tears, she walked from the room, carefully drawing her dress aside as Gunn held the door for her.

"A fine girl," said Gunn, his thin lips working; "a fine spirit. 'Twill be pleasant to break it; but she does not know who is master here."

"She is young yet," said the other, hurriedly.

"I will soon age her if she looks like that at me again," said Gunn. "By ——, I'll turn out the whole crew into the street, and her with them, an' I wish it. I'll lie in my bed warm o' nights and think of her huddled on a doorstep."

His voice rose and his fists clenched, but he kept his distance and watched the other warily. The innkeeper's face was contorted and his brow grew wet. For one moment something peeped out of his eyes; the next he sat down in his chair again and nervously fingered his chin.

"I have but to speak," said Gunn, regarding him with much satisfaction, "and you will hang, and your money go to the Crown. What will become of her then, think you?"

The other laughed nervously.

"'Twould be stopping the golden eggs," he ventured.

"Don't think too much of that," said Gunn, in a hard voice. "I was never one to be baulked, as you know."

"Come, come. Let us be friends," said Mullet; "the girl is young, and has had her way."

He looked almost pleadingly at the other, and his voice trembled. Gunn drew himself up, and regarding him with a satisfied sneer, quitted the room without a word.

Affairs at the "Golden Key" grew steadily worse and worse. Gunn dominated the place, and his vile personality hung over it like a shadow. Appeals to the innkeeper were in vain; his health was breaking fast, and he moodily declined to interfere. Gunn appointed servants of his own choosing—brazen maids and foul-mouthed men. The old patrons ceased to frequent the "Golden

Key," and its bedrooms stood empty. The maids scarcely deigned to take an order from Joan, and the men spoke to her familiarly. In the midst of all this the innkeeper, who had complained once or twice of vertigo, was seized with a fit.

Joan, flying to him for protection against the brutal advances of Gunn, found him lying in a heap behind the door of his small office, and in her fear called loudly for assistance. A little knot of servants collected, and stood regarding him stupidly. One made a brutal jest. Gunn, pressing through the throng, turned the senseless body over with his foot, and cursing vilely, ordered them to carry it upstairs.

Until the surgeon came, Joan, kneeling by the bed, held on to the senseless hand as her only protection against the evil faces of Gunn and his protégés. Gunn himself was taken aback, the innkeeper's death at that time by no means suiting his aims.

The surgeon was a man of few words and fewer attainments, but under his ministrations the innkeeper, after a long interval, rallied. The half-closed eyes opened, and he looked in a dazed fashion at his surroundings. Gunn drove the servants away and questioned the man of medicine. The answers were vague and interspersed with Latin. Freedom from noise and troubles of all kinds was insisted upon and Joan was installed as nurse, with a promise of speedy assistance.

The assistance arrived late in the day in the shape of an elderly woman, whose Spartan treatment of her patients had helped many along the silent road. She commenced her reign by punching the sick man's pillows, and having shaken him into consciousness by this means, gave him a dose of physic, after first tasting it herself from the bottle.

After the first rally the innkeeper began to fail slowly. It was seldom that he understood what was said to him, and pitiful to the beholder to see in his intervals of consciousness his timid anxiety to earn the good-will of the all-powerful Gunn. His strength declined until assistance was needed to turn him in the bed, and his great sinewy hands were forever trembling and fidgeting on the coverlet.

Joan, pale with grief and fear, tended him assiduously. Her stepfather's strength had been a proverb in the town, and many a hasty citizen had felt the strength of his arm. The increasing lawlessness of the house filled her with dismay, and the coarse attentions of Gunn became more persistent than ever. She took her meals in the sick-room, and divided her time between that and her own.

Gunn himself was in a dilemma. With Mullet dead, his power was at an end and his visions of wealth dissipated. He resolved to feather his nest immediately, and interviewed the surgeon. The surgeon was ominously reticent, the nurse cheerfully ghoulish.

"Four days I give him," she said, calmly; "four blessed days, not but what he might slip away at any moment."

Gunn let one day of the four pass, and then, choosing a time when Joan was from the room, entered it for a little quiet conversation. The innkeeper's eyes were open, and, what was more to the purpose, intelligent.

"You're cheating the hangman, after all," snarled Gunn. "I'm off to swear an information."

The other, by a great effort, turned his heavy head and fixed his wistful eyes on him.

"Mercy!" he whispered. "For her sake—give me—a little time!"

"To slip your cable, I suppose," quoth Gunn. "Where's your money? Where's your hoard, you miser?"

Mullet closed his eyes. He opened them again slowly and strove to think, while Gunn watched him narrowly. When he spoke, his utterance was thick and labored.

"Come to-night," he muttered, slowly. "Give me—time—I will make your—your fortune. But the nurse—watches."

"I'll see to her," said Gunn, with a grin. "But tell me now, lest you die first."

"You will—let Joan—have a share?" panted the innkeeper.

"Yes, yes," said Gunn, hastily.

The innkeeper strove to raise himself in the bed, and then fell back again exhausted as Joan's step was heard on the stairs. Gunn gave a savage glance of warning at him, and barring the progress of the girl at the door, attempted to salute her. Joan came in pale and trembling, and falling on her knees by the bedside, took her father's hand in hers and wept over it. The innkeeper gave a faint groan and a shiver ran through his body.

It was nearly an hour after midnight that Nick Gunn, kicking off his shoes, went stealthily out onto the landing. A little light came from the partly open door of the sick-room, but all else was in blackness. He moved along and peered in.

The nurse was sitting in a high-backed oak chair by the fire. She had slipped down in the seat, and her untidy head hung on her bosom. A glass stood on the small oak table by her side, and a solitary candle on the high mantel-piece diffused a sickly light. Gunn entered the room, and finding that the sick man was dozing, shook him roughly.

The innkeeper opened his eyes and gazed at him blankly.

"Wake, you fool," said Gunn, shaking him again.

The other roused and muttered something incoherently. Then he stirred slightly.

"The nurse," he whispered.

"She's safe enow," said Gunn. "I've seen to that."

He crossed the room lightly, and standing before the unconscious woman, inspected her closely and raised her in the chair. Her head fell limply over the arm.

"Dead?" inquired Mullet, in a fearful whisper.

"Drugged," said Gunn, shortly. "Now speak up, and be lively."

The innkeeper's eyes again travelled in the direction of the nurse.

"The men," he whispered; "the servants."

"Dead drunk and asleep," said Gunn, biting the words. "The last day would hardly rouse them. Now will you speak, damn you!"

"I must—take care—of Joan," said the father.

Gunn shook his clenched hand at him.

"My money—is—is—" said the other. "Promise me on—your oath—Joan."

"Ay, ay," growled Gunn; "how many more times? I'll marry her, and she shall have what I choose to give her. Speak up, you fool! It's not for you to make terms. Where is it?"

He bent over, but Mullet, exhausted with his efforts, had closed his eyes again, and half turned his head.

"Where is it, damn you?" said Gunn, from between his teeth.

Mullet opened his eyes again, glanced fearfully round the room, and whispered. Gunn, with a stifled oath, bent his ear almost to his mouth, and the next moment his neck was in the grip of the strongest man in Riverstone, and an arm like a bar of iron over his back pinned him down across the bed.

"You dog!" hissed a fierce voice in his ear. "I've got you—Captain Rogers at your service, and now you may tell his name to all you can. Shout it, you spawn of hell. Shout it!"

He rose in bed, and with a sudden movement flung the other over on his back. Gunn's eyes were starting from his head, and he writhed convulsively.

"I thought you were a sharper man, Gunn," said Rogers, still in the same hot whisper, as he relaxed his grip a little; "you are too simple, you hound! When you first threatened me I resolved to kill you. Then you threatened my daughter. I wish that you had nine lives, that I might take them all. Keep still!"

He gave a half-glance over his shoulder at the silent figure of the nurse, and put his weight on the twisting figure on the bed.

"You drugged the hag, good Gunn," he continued. "To-morrow morning, Gunn, they will find you in your room dead, and if one of the scum you brought into my house be charged with the murder, so much the better. When I am well they will go. I am already feeling a little bit stronger, Gunn, as you see, and in a month I hope to be about again."

He averted his face, and for a time gazed sternly and watchfully at the door. Then he rose slowly to his feet, and taking the dead man in his arms, bore him slowly and carefully to his room, and laid him a huddled heap on the floor. Swiftly and noiselessly he put the dead man's shoes on and turned his pockets inside out, kicked a rug out of place, and put a guinea on the floor. Then he stole cautiously downstairs and set a small door at the back open. A dog barked frantically, and he hurried back to his room. The nurse still slumbered by the fire.

She awoke in the morning shivering with the cold, and being jealous of her reputation, rekindled the fire, and measuring out the dose which the invalid should have taken, threw it away. On these unconscious preparations for an alibi Captain Rogers gazed through half-closed lids, and then turning his grim face to the wall, waited for the inevitable alarm.

To Build a Fire

Jack London

Day had broken cold and gray, exceedingly cold and gray, when the man turned aside from the main Yukon trail and climbed the high earth-bank, where a dim and little-travelled trail led eastward through the fat spruce timberland. It was a steep bank, and he paused for breath at the top, excusing the act to himself by looking at his watch. It was nine o'clock. There was no sun nor hind of sun, though there was not a cloud in the sky. It was a clear day, and yet there seemed an intangible pall over the face of things, a subtle gloom that made the day dark, and that was due to the absence of sun. This fact did not worry the man. He was used to the lack of sun. It had been days since he had seen the sun, and he knew that a few more days must pass before that cheerful orb, due south, would just peep above the sky line and dip immediately from view.

The man flung a look back along the way he had come. The Yukon lay a mile wide and hidden under three feet of ice. On top of this ice were as many feet of snow. It was all pure white, rolling in gentle undulations where the ice jams of the freeze-up had formed. North and south, as far as his eye could see, it was unbroken white, save for a dark hairline that curved and twisted from around the spruce-covered island to the south, and that curved and twisted away into the north, where it disappeared behind another spruce-covered island. This dark hairline was the trail—the main trail—that led south five hundred miles to the Chilcoot Pass, Dyea, and salt water; and that led north seventy miles to Dawson, and still on to the north a thousand miles to Nulato, and finally to St. Michael, on Bearing Sea, a thousand miles and half a thousand more.

But all this—the mysterious, far-reaching hairline trail, the absence of sun from the sky, the tremendous cold, and the strangeness and weirdness of it all—made no impression on the man. It was not because he was long used to it. He was a newcomer in the land, a "chechaquo," and this was his first winter. The trouble with him was that he was without imagination. He was quick and alert in the things of life, but only in the things, and not in the significances. Fifty degrees below zero meant eighty odd degrees of frost. Such fact impressed him as being cold and uncomfortable, and that was all. It did not lead him to meditate upon his frailty in general, able only to live within certain narrow limits of heat and cold; and from there on it did not lead him to the conjectural field of immortality and man's place in the universe. Fifty degrees below zero stood for a bite of frost that hurt and that must be guarded against by the use of mittens, ear flaps, warm moccasins, and thick socks. Fifty degrees below zero was to him just precisely fifty degrees below zero. That there should be anything more to it than that was a thought that never entered his head.

As he turned to go, he spat speculatively. There was a sharp, explosive crackle that startled him. He spat again. And again, in the air, before it could fall to the snow, the spittle crackled. He knew that at fifty below spittle crackled on the snow, but this spittle had crackled in the air. Undoubtedly it was colder than fifty below—how much colder he did not know. But the temperature did not matter. He was bound for the old claim on the left fork of Henderson Creek, where the boys were already. They had come over across the divide from the Indian Creek country, while he had come the roundabout way to take a look at the possibility of getting out logs in the spring from the islands in the Yukon. He would be in to camp by six o'clock; a bit after dark, it was true, but the boys would be there, a fire would be going, and a hot supper would be ready. As for lunch, he pressed his hand against the protruding bundle under his jacket. It was also under his shirt, wrapped up in a handkerchief and lying against the naked skin. It was the only way to keep the biscuits from freezing. He smiled agreeably to himself as he thought of those biscuits, each cut open and sopped in bacon grease, and each enclosing a generous slice of fried bacon.

He plunged in among the big spruce trees. The trail was faint.

A foot of snow had fallen since the last sled had passed over, and he was glad he was without a sled, travelling light. In fact, he carried nothing but the lunch wrapped in the handkerchief. He was surprised, however, at the cold. It certainly was cold, he concluded, as he rubbed his numb nose and cheekbones with his mittened hand. He was a warm-whiskered man, but the hair on his face did not protect the high cheekbones and the eager nose that thrust itself aggressively into the frosty air.

At the man's heels trotted a dog, a big native husky, the proper wolf dog, gray-coated and without any visible or temperamental difference from its brother, the wild wolf. The animal was depressed by the tremendous cold. It knew that it was no time for travelling. Its instinct told it a truer tale than was told to the man by the man's judgment. In reality, it was not merely colder than fifty below zero; it was colder than sixty below, than seventy below. It was seventy-five below zero. Since the freezing point is thirty-two above zero, it meant that one hundred and seven degrees of frost obtained. The dog did not know anything about thermometers. Possibly in its brain there was no sharp consciousness of a condition of very cold such as was in the man's brain. But the brute had its instinct. It experienced a vague but menacing apprehension that subdued it and made it slink along at the man's heels, and that made it question eagerly every unwonted movement of the man as if expecting him to go into camp or to seek shelter somewhere and build a fire. The dog had learned fire and it wanted fire, or else to burrow under the snow and cuddle its warmth away from the air

The frozen moisture of its (i.e., the dog's) breathing had settled on its fur in a fine powder of frost, and especially were its jowls, muzzle, and eyelashes whitened by its crystalled breath. The man's red beard and mustache were likewise frosted, but more solidly, the deposit taking the form of ice and increasing with every warm, moist breath he exhaled. Also, the man was chewing tobacco and the muzzle of ice held his lips so rigidly that he was unable to clear his chin when he expelled the juice. The result was that a crystal beard of the color and solidity of amber was increasing its length on his chin. If he fell down it would shatter itself, like glass, into brittle fragments. But he did not mind the appendage. It was the penalty all tobacco chewers paid in that country, and he had been out before in two cold snaps. They had not been so cold as this, he knew, but by the spirit thermometer at Sixty Mile he knew they had registered at fifty below and at fifty-five.

He held on through the level stretch of woods for several miles, crossed a wide flat of nigger heads, and dropped down a bank to the frozen bed of a small stream. This was Henderson Creek, and he knew he was ten miles from the forks. He looked at his watch. It was ten o'clock. He was making four miles an hour, and he calculated that he would arrive at the forks at half-past twelve. He decided to celebrate that event by eating his lunch there.

The dog dropped in again at his heels, with a tail drooping discouragement, as the man sung along the creek bed. The furrow of the old sled trail was plainly visible, but a dozen inches of snow covered the marks of the last runners. In a month no man had come up or down that silent creek. The man held steadily on. He was not much given to thinking, and just then particularly he had nothing to think about save that he would eat lunch at the forks and that at six o'clock he would be in camp with the boys. There was nobody to talk to; and, had there been, speech would have been impossible because of the ice muzzle on his mouth. So he continued monotonously to chew tobacco and to increase the length of his amber beard.

Once in a while the thought reiterated itself that it was very cold and that he had never experienced such cold. As he walked along he rubbed his cheekbones and nose with the back of his mittened hand. He did this automatically, now and again changing hands. But, rub as he would, the instant he stopped his cheekbones went numb, and the following instant the end of his nose went numb. He was sure to frost his cheeks; he knew that, and experienced a pang of regret that he had not devised a nose strap of the sort Bud wore in cold snaps. Such a strap passed across the cheeks, as well, and saved them. But it didn't matter much, after all. What were frosted cheeks? A bit painful, that was all; they were never serious.

Empty as the man's mind was of thoughts, he was keenly observant, and he noticed the changes in the creek, the curves and bends and timber jams, and always he sharply noted where he placed his feet. Once, coming around a bend, he shied abruptly, like a startled horse, curved away from the place where he had been walking, and retreated several paces back along the trail. The creek he knew was frozen clear to the bottom—no creek could contain water in that arctic winter—but he knew also that there were springs that bubbled out from the hillsides and ran along under the snow and on top the ice of the creek. He knew that the coldest snaps never froze these springs, and he knew likewise their danger. They were traps. They hid pools of water under the snow that might be three inches deep, or three feet. Sometimes a skin of ice half an inch thick covered them, and in turn was covered by the snow. Sometimes there were alternate layers of water and ice skin, so that when one broke through he kept on breaking through for a while, sometimes wetting himself to the waist.

That was why he had shied in such panic. He had felt the give under his feet and heard the crackle of a snow-hidden ice skin. And to get his feet wet in such a temperature meant trouble and danger. At the very least it meant delay, for he would be forced to stop and build a fire, and under its protection to bare his feet while he dried his socks and moccasins. He stood and studied the creek bed and its banks, and decided that the flow of water came from the right. He reflected awhile, rubbing his nose and cheeks, then skirted to the left, stepping gingerly and testing the footing for each step. Once clear of the danger, he took a fresh chew of tobacco and swung along at his four-mile gait. The danger of falling through the ice had become a factor.

In the course of the next two hours he came upon several similar traps. Usually the snow above the hidden pools had a sunken, candied appearance that advertised the danger. Once again, however, he had a close call; and once, suspecting danger, he compelled the dog to go on in front. The dog did not want to go. It hung back until the man shoved it forward, and then it went quickly across the white, unbroken surface. Suddenly it broke through, floundered to one side, and got away to firmer footing. It had wet its forefeet and legs, and almost immediately the water that clung to it turned to ice. It made quick efforts to lick the ice off its legs, then dropped down in the snow and began to bite out the ice that had formed between the toes. This was a matter of instinct. To permit the ice to remain would mean sore feet. It did not know this. It merely obeyed the mysterious prompting that arose from the deep crypts of its being. But the man knew, having achieved a judgment on the subject, and he removed the mitten from his right hand and helped tear out the ice particles. He did not expose his fingers more than a minute, and was astonished at the swift numbness that smote them. It certainly was cold. He pulled on the mitten hastily, and beat the hand savagely across his chest.

At twelve o'clock the day was at its brightest. Yet the sun was too far south on its winter journey to clear the horizon. The bulge of the earth intervened between it and Henderson Creek, where the man walked under a clear sky at noon and cast no shadow. At half-past twelve, to the minute, he arrived at the forks of the creek. He was pleased at the speed he had made. If he kept it up, he would certainly be with the boys by six. He unbuttoned his jacket and shirt and drew forth his lunch. The action consumed no more than a quarter of a minute, yet in that brief moment the numbness laid hold of his exposed fingers. He did not put the mitten on, but, instead, struck the fingers a dozen sharp smashes against his leg. Then he sat down on a snow-covered log to eat. The sting that followed upon the striking of his fingers against his leg ceased so quickly that he was startled. He had had no chance to take a bit of biscuit. He struck the fingers repeatedly and returned them to the mitten, baring the other hand for the purpose of eating. He tried to take a mouthful, but the ice muzzle prevented. He had forgotten to build a fire and thaw out. He chuckled at his foolishness, and as he chuckled he noted that the stinging which had first come to his toes when he sat down was already passing away. He wondered whether the toes were warm or numb. He moved them inside the moccasins and decided that they were numb.

He pulled the mitten on hurriedly and stood up. He was a bit frightened. He stamped up and down until the stinging returned to his feet. It certainly was cold, was his thought. That man from Sulphur Creek had spoken the truth when telling how cold it sometimes got in the country. And he had laughed at him at the time! That showed one must not be too sure of things. There was no mistake about it, it *was* cold. He strode up and down, stamping his feet and threshing his arms, until reassured by the returning warmth. Then he got out matches and proceeded to make a fire.

From the undergrowth, where high water of the previous spring had lodged a supply of seasoned twigs, he got his firewood. Working carefully from a small beginning, he soon had a roaring fire, over which he thawed the ice from his face and in the protection of which he ate his biscuits. For the moment the cold of space was outwitted. The dog took satisfaction in the fire, stretching out close enough for warmth and far enough away to escape being singed.

When the man had finished, he filled his pipe and took his comfortable time over a smoke. Then he pulled on his mittens, settled the ear flaps of his cap firmly about his ears, and took the creek trail up the left fork. The dog was disappointed and yearned back toward the fire. The man did not know cold. Possibly all the generations of his ancestry had been ignorant of cold, of real cold, of cold one hundred and seven degrees below freezing point. But the dog knew; all its ancestry knew, and it had inherited the knowledge. And it knew that it was not good to walk abroad in such fearful cold. It was the time to lie snug in a hole in the snow and wait for a curtain of cloud to be drawn across the face of outer space whence this cold came. On the other hand, there was no keen intimacy between the dog and the man. The one was the toil slave of the other, and the only caresses it had ever received were the caresses of the whip lash and of harsh and menacing throat sounds that threatened the whip lash. So the dog made no effort to communicate its apprehension to the man. It was not concerned in the welfare of the man; it was for its own sake that it yearned back toward the fire. But the man whistled, and spoke to it with the sound of whip lashes, and the dog swung in at the man's heels and followed after.

The man took a chew of tobacco and proceeded to start a new amber beard. Also, his moist breath quickly powdered with white his mustache, eyebrows, and lashes. There did not seem to be so many springs on the left fork of the Henderson, and for half an hour the man saw no signs of any. And then it happened. At a place where there were no signs, where the soft, unbroken snow seemed to advertise solidity beneath, the man broke through. It was not deep. He wet himself halfway to the knees before he floundered out to the firm crust.

He was angry, and cursed his luck aloud. He had hoped to get into camp with the boys at six o'clock, and this would delay him an hour, for he would have to build a fire and dry out his footgear. This was imperative at that low temperature—for he knew that much; and he turned aside to the bank, which he climbed. On top, tangled in the underbrush about the trunks of several small spruce trees, was a high water deposit of dry firewood—sticks and twigs, principally, but also larger portions of seasoned branches and fine, dry, last year's grasses. He threw down several large pieces on top of the snow. This served for a foundation and prevented the young flame from drowning itself in the snow it otherwise would melt. The flame he got by touching a match to a small shred of birch bark that he took from his pocket. This burned even more readily than paper. Placing it on the foundation, he fed the young flame with wisps of dry grass and with the tiniest dry twigs.

He worked slowly and carefully, keenly aware of his danger. Gradually, as the flame grew stronger, he increased the size of the twigs with which he fed it. He squatted in the snow, pulling the twigs out from their entanglement in the brush and feeding directly to the flame. He knew there must be no failure. When it is seventy-five below zero, a man must not fail in his first attempt to build a fire—that is, if his feet are wet. If his feet are dry, and he fails, he can run along the trail for half a mile and restore his circulation. But the circulation of wet and freezing feet cannot be restored by running when it is seventy-five below. No matter how fast he runs, the wet feet will freeze the harder.

All this the man knew. The old-timer on Sulphur Creek had told him about it the previous fall, and now he was appreciating the advice. Already all sensation had gone out of his feet. To build the fire he had been forced to remove his mittens, and the fingers had quickly gone numb. His pace of four miles an hour had kept his heart pumping blood to the surface of his body and to all the extremities. But the instant he stopped, the action of the pump eased down. The cold of space smote the unprotected tip of the planet, and he, being on that unprotected tip, received the full force of the blow. The blood of his body recoiled before it. The blood was alive, like the dog, and like the dog it wanted to hide away and cover itself up from the fearful cold. So long as he walked four miles an hour, he pumped that blood, willy-nilly, to the surface; but now it ebbed away and sank down into the recesses of his body. The extremities were the first to feel its absence. His wet feet froze the faster, and his exposed fingers numbed the faster, though they had not yet begun to freeze. Nose and cheeks were already freezing, while the skin of all his body chilled as it lost its blood.

But he was safe. Toes and nose and cheeks would be only touched by the frost, for the fire was beginning to burn with strength. He was feeding it with twigs the size of his finger. In another minute he would be able to feed it with branches the size of his wrist, and then he could remove his wet footgear, and, while it dried, he could keep his naked feet warm by the fire, rubbing them at first, of course, with snow. The fire was a success. He was safe. He remembered the advice of the old-timer on Sulphur Creek, and smiled. The old-timer had been very serious in laying down the law that no man must travel alone in the Klondike after fifty below. Well, here he was; he had had the accident; he was alone; and he had saved himself. Those old-timers were rather womanish, some of them, he thought. All a man had to do was to keep his head, and he was all right. Any man who was a man could travel alone. But it was surprising, the rapidity with which his cheeks and nose were freezing. And he had not thought his fingers could go lifeless in so short a time. Lifeless they were, for he could scarcely make them move together to grip a twig, and they seemed remote from his body and from him. When he touched a twig, he had to look and see whether or not he had hold of it. The wires were pretty well down between him and his finger ends.

All of which counted for little. There was the fire, snapping and crackling and promising life with every dancing flame. He started to untie his moccasins. They were coated with ice; the thick German socks were like sheaths of iron halfway to the knees; and the moccasin strings were like rods of steel all twisted and knotted as by some conflagration. For a moment he tugged with his numb fingers, then, realizing the folly of it, he drew his sheath knife.

But before he could cut the strings, it happened. It was his own fault or, rather, his mistake. He should not have built the fire under the spruce tree. He should have built it in the open. But it had been easier to pull the twigs from the brush and drop them directly on the fire. Now the tree under which he had done this carried a weight of snow on its boughs. No wind had blown for weeks, and each bough was fully freighted. Each time he had pulled on a twig he had communicated a slight agitation to the tree—an imperceptible agitation, so far as he was concerned, but an agitation sufficient to bring about the disaster. High up in the tree one bough capsized its load of snow. This fell on the boughs beneath, capsizing them. This process continued, spreading out and involving the whole tree. It grew like an avalanche, and it descended without warning upon the man and the fire, and the fire was blotted out! Where it had burned was a mantle of fresh and disordered snow.

The man was shocked. It was as though he had just heard his own sentence of death. For a moment he sat and stared at the spot where the fire had been. Then he grew very calm. Perhaps the old-timer on Sulphur Creek was right. If he had only had a trail mate he would have been in no danger now. The trail mate could have built the fire. Well, it was up to him to build a fire over again, and this second time there must be no failure. Even if he succeeded, he would most likely lose some toes. His feet must be badly frozen by now, and there would be some time before the second fire was ready.

Such were his thoughts, but he did not sit and think them. He was busy all the time they were passing through his mind. He made a new foundation for a fire, this time in the open, where no treacherous tree could blot it out. Next he gathered dry grasses and tiny twigs from the high water flotsam. He could not bring his fingers together to pull them out, but he was able to gather them by the handful. In this way he got many rotten twigs and bits of green moss that were undesirable, but it was the best he could do. He worked methodically, even collecting an armful of the larger branches to be used later when the fire gathered strength. And all the while the dog sat and watched him, a certain yearning wistfulness in its eyes, for it looked upon him as the fire provider, and the fire was slow in coming.

When all was ready, the man reached in his pocket for a second piece of birch bark. He knew the bark was there, and, though he could not feel it with his fingers, he could hear its crisp rustling as he fumbled for it. Try as he would, he could not clutch hold of it. And all the time, in his consciousness, was the knowledge that each instant his feet were freezing. This thought tended to put him in a panic, but he fought against it and kept calm. He pulled on his mittens with his teeth, and thrashed his arms back and forth, beating his hands with all his might against his sides. He did this sitting down, and he stood up to do it; and all the while the dog sat in the snow, its wolf brush of a tail curled around warmly over its forefeet, its sharp wolf ears pricked forward intently as it watched the man. And the man, as he beat and threshed with his arms and hands, felt a great surge of envy as he regarded the creature that was warm and secure in its natural covering.

After a time he was aware of the first faraway signals of sensation in his beaten fingers. The faint tingling grew stronger till it evolved into a stinging ache that was excruciating, but which the man hailed with satisfaction. He stripped the mitten from his right hand and fetched forth the birch bark. The exposed fingers were quickly going numb again. Next he brought out his bunch of sulphur matches. But the tremendous cold had already driven the life out of his fingers. In his effort to separate one match from the others, the whole bunch fell in the snow. He tried to pick it out of the snow, but failed. The dead fingers could neither touch nor clutch. He was very careful. He drove the thought of his freezing feet, and nose, and cheeks, out of his mind, devoting his whole soul to the matches. He watched, using the sense of vision in place of that of touch, and when he saw his fingers on each side the bunch, he closed them—that is, he willed to close them, for the wires were down, and the fingers did not obey. He pulled the mitten on the right hand, and beat it fiercely against his knee. Then, with both mittened hands, he scooped the bunch of matches, along with much snow, into his lap. Yet he was no better off.

After some manipulation he managed to get the bunch between the heels of his mittened hands. In this fashion he carried it to his mouth. The ice crackled and snapped when by a violent effort he opened his mouth. He drew the lower jaw in, curled the upper lip out of the way, and scraped the bunch with his upper teeth in order to separate a match. He succeeded in getting one, which he dropped on his lap. He was no better off. He could not pick it up. Then he devised a way. He picked it up in his teeth and scratched it on his leg. Twenty times he scratched before he succeeded in lighting it. As if flamed he held it with his teeth to the birch bark. But the burning brimstone went up his nostrils and into his lungs, causing him to cough spasmodically. The match fell into the snow and went out.

The old-timer on Sulphur Creek was right, he thought in the moment of controlled despair that ensued: after fifty below, a man should travel with a partner. He beat his hands, but failed in exciting any sensation. Suddenly he bared both hands, removing the mittens with his teeth. He caught the whole bunch between the heels of his hands. His arm muscles not being frozen enabled him to press the hand heels tightly against the matches. Then he scratched the bunch along his leg. It flared into flame, seventy sulphur matches at once! There was no wind to blow them out. He kept his head to one side to escape the strangling fumes, and held the blazing bundle to the birch bark. As he so held it, he became aware of sensation in his hand. His flesh was burning. He could smell it. Deep down below the surface he could feel it. The sensation developed into pain that grew acute. And still he endured it, holding the flame of the matches clumsily to the bark that would not light readily because his own burning hands were in the way, absorbing most of the flame.

At last, when he could endure no more, he jerked his hands apart. The blazing matches fell sizzling into the snow, but the birch bark was alight. He began laying dry grasses and the tiniest twigs on the flame. He could not pick and choose, for he had to lift the fuel between the heels of his hands. Small pieces of rotten wood and green moss clung to the twigs, and he bit them off as well as he could with his teeth. He cherished the flame carefully and awkwardly. It meant life, and it must not perish. The withdrawal of blood from the surface of his body now made him begin to shiver, and he grew more awkward. A large piece of green moss fell squarely on the little fire. He tried to poke it with his fingers, but his shivering frame made him poke too far, and he disrupted the nucleus of the little fire, the burning grasses and tiny twigs separating and scattering. He tried to poke them together again, but in spite of the tenseness of the effort, his shivering got away with him, and the twigs were hopelessly scattered. Each twig gushed a puff of smoke and went out. The fire provider had failed. As he looked apathetically about him, his eyes chanced on the dog, sitting across the ruins of the fire from him, in the snow, making restless, hunching movements, slightly lifting one forefoot and then the other, shifting its weight back and forth on them with wistful eagerness.

The sight of the dog put a wild idea into his head. He remembered the tale of the man, caught in a blizzard, who killed a steer and crawled inside the carcass, and so was saved. He would kill the dog and bury his hands in the warm body until the numbness went out of them. Then he could build another fire. He spoke to the dog, calling it to him; but in his voice was a strange note of fear that frightened the animal, who had never known the man to speak in such a way before. Something was the matter, and its suspicious nature sensed danger-it knew not what danger, but somewhere, somehow, in its brain arose an apprehension of the man. It flattened its ears down at the sound of the man's voice, and its restless, hunching movements and liftings and shiftings of its forefeet became more pronounced; but it would not come to the man. He got on his hands and knees and crawled toward the dog. This unusual posture again excited suspicion, and the animal sidled mincingly away.

The man sat up in the snow for a moment and struggled for calmness. Then he pulled on his mittens, by means of his teeth, and got upon his feet. He glanced down at first in order to assure himself that he was really standing up, for the absence of sensation in his feet left him unrelated to the earth. His erect position in itself started to drive the webs of suspicion from the dog's mind; and when he spoke peremptorily, with the sound of whip lashes in his voice, the dog rendered its customary allegiance and came to him. As it came within reaching distance, the man lost his control. His arms flashed out to the dog, and he experienced genuine surprise when he discovered that his hands could not clutch, that there was neither bend nor feeling in the fingers. He had forgotten for the moment that they were frozen and that they were freezing more and more. All this happened quickly, and before the animal could get away, he encircled its body with his arms. He sat down in the snow, and in this fashion held the dog, while it snarled and whined and struggled.

But it was all he could do, hold its body encircled in his arms and sit there. He realized that he could not kill the dog. There was no way to do it. With his helpless hands he could neither draw nor hold his sheath knife nor throttle the animal. He released it, and it plunged wildly away, with tail between its legs, and still snarling. It halted forty feet away surveyed him curiously, with ears sharply pricked forward.

The man looked down at his hands in order to locate them, and found them hanging on the ends of his arms. It struck him as curious that one should have to use his eyes in order to find out where his hands were. He began threshing his arms back and forth, beating the mittened hands against his sides. He did this for five minutes, violently, and his heart pumped enough blood up to the surface to put a stop to his shivering. But no sensation was aroused in his hands. He had an impression that they hung like weights on the ends of his arms, but when he tried to run the impression down, he could not find it.

A certain fear of death, dull and oppressive, came to him. This fear quickly became poignant as he realized that it was no longer a mere matter of freezing his fingers and toes, or of losing his hands and feet, but that it was a matter of life and death with the chances against him. This threw him into a panic, and he turned and ran up the creek bed along the old, dim trail. The dog joined in behind and kept up with him. He ran blindly, without intention, in fear such as he had never known in his life.

Slowly, as he plowed and floundered through the snow, he began to see things again—the banks of the creek, the old timber jams, the leafless aspens, and the sky. The running made him feel better. He did not shiver. Maybe, if he ran on, his feet would thaw out; and, anyway, if he ran far enough, he would reach camp and the boys. Without doubt he would lose some fingers and toes and some of his face; but the boys would take care of him, and save the rest of him when he got there. And at the same time there was another thought in his mind that said he would never get to the camp and the boys; that it was too many miles away, that the freezing had too great a start on him, and that he would soon be stiff and dead. This thought he kept in the background and refused to consider. Sometimes it pushed itself forward and demanded to be heard, but he thrust it back and strove to think of other things.

It struck him as curious that he could run at all on feet so frozen that he could not feel them when they struck the earth and took the weight of his body. He seemed to himself to skim along above the surface, and to have no connection with the earth. Somewhere he had once seen a winged Mercury, and he wondered if Mercury felt as he felt when skimming over the earth.

His theory of running until he reached camp and the boys had one flaw in it; he lacked the endurance. Several times he stumbled, and finally he tottered, crumpled up, and fell. When he tried to rise, he failed. He must sit and rest, he decided, and next time he would merely walk and keep on going. As he sat and regained his breath, he noted that he was feeling quite warm and comfortable. He was not shivering, and it even seemed that a warm glow had come to his chest and trunk. And yet, when he touched his nose or cheeks, there was no sensation. Running would not thaw them out. Nor would it thaw out his hands and feet. Then the thought came to him that the frozen portions of his body must be extending. He tried to keep this thought down, to forget it, to think of something else; he was aware of the panicky feeling that it caused, and he was afraid of the panic. But the thought asserted itself, and persisted, until it produced a vision of his body totally frozen. This was too much, and he made another wild run along the trail. Once he slowed down to a walk, but the thought of the freezing extending itself made him run again.

And all the time the dog ran with him, at his heels. When he fell down a second time, it curled its tail over its forefeet and sat in front of him, facing him, curiously eager and intent. The warmth and security of the animal angered him, and he cursed it till it flattened down its ears appeasingly. This time the shivering came more quickly upon the man. He was losing his battle with the frost. It was creeping into his body from all sides. The thought of it drove him on, but he ran no more than a hundred feet, when he staggered and pitched headlong. It was his last panic. When he had recovered his breath and control, he sat up and entertained in his mind the conception of meeting death with dignity. However, the conception did not come to him in such terms. His idea of it was that he had been making a fool of himself, running around like a chicken with its head cut off—such was the simile that occurred to him. Well, he was bound to freeze anyway, and he might as well take it decently. With this new-found peace of mind came the first glimmerings of drowsiness. A good idea, he thought, to sleep off to death. It was like taking an anesthetic. Freezing was not so bad a people thought. There were lots worse ways to die.

He pictured the boys finding his body next day. Suddenly he found himself with them, coming along the trail and looking for himself. And, still with them, he came around a turn in the trail and found himself lying in the snow. He did not belong with himself any more, for even then he was out of himself, standing with the boys and looking at himself in the snow. It certainly was cold, was his thought. When he got back to the States he could tell the folks what real cold was. He drifted on from this to a vision of the old-timer on Sulphur Creek. He could see him quite clearly, warm and comfortable, and smoking a pipe.

Then the man drowsed off into what seemed to him the most comfortable and satisfying sleep he had ever known. The dog sat facing and waiting. The brief day drew to a close in a long, slow twilight. There were no signs of a fire to be made, and, besides, never in the dog's experience had it known a man to sit like that in the snow and make no fire. As the twilight drew on, its eager yearning for the fire mastered it, and with a great lifting and shifting of forefeet, it whined softly, then flattened out its ears down in anticipation of being chidden by the man. But the man remained silent. Later the dog whined loudly. And still later it crept close to the man and caught the scent of death. This made the animal bristle and back away. A little longer it delayed, howling under the stars that leaped and danced and shone brightly in the cold sky. Then it turned and trotted up the trail in the direction of the camp it knew, where were the other food providers and fire providers.

Leiningen versus the Ants

Carl Stephenson

Unless they alter their course and there's no reason why they should, they'll reach your plantation in two days at the latest."

Leiningen sucked placidly at a cigar about the size of a corncob and for a few seconds gazed without answering at the agitated District Commissioner. Then he took the cigar from his lips, and leaned slightly forward. With his bristling grey hair, bulky nose, and lucid eyes, he had the look of an aging and shabby eagle.

"Decent of you," he murmured, "paddling all this way just to give me the tip. But you're pulling my leg of course when you say I must do a bunk. Why, even a herd of saurians couldn't drive me from this plantation of mine."

The Brazilian official threw up lean and lanky arms and clawed the air with wildly distended fingers. "Leiningen!" he shouted. "You're insane! They're not creatures you can fight—they're an elemental—an 'act of God!' Ten miles long, two miles wide—ants, nothing but ants! And every single one of them a fiend from hell; before you can spit three times they'll eat a full-grown buffalo to the bones. I tell you if you don't clear out at once there'll he nothing left of you but a skeleton picked as clean as your own plantation."

Leiningen grinned. "Act of God, my eye! Anyway, I'm not an old woman; I'm not going to run for it just because an elemental's on the way. And don't think I'm the kind of fathead who tries to fend off lightning with his fists either. I use my intelligence, old man. With me, the brain isn't a second blindgut; I know what it's there for. When I began this model farm and plantation three years ago, I took into account all that could conceivably happen to it. And now I'm ready for anything and everything—including your ants."

The Brazilian rose heavily to his feet. "I've done my best," he gasped. "Your obstinacy endangers not only yourself, but the lives of your four hundred workers. You don't know these ants!"

Leiningen accompanied him down to the river, where the Government launch was moored. The vessel cast off. As it moved downstream, the exclamation mark neared the rail and began waving its arms frantically. Long after the launch had disappeared round the bend, Leiningen thought he could still hear that dimming imploring voice, "You don't know them, I tell you! You don't know them!"

But the reported enemy was by no means unfamiliar to the planter. Before he started work on his settlement, he had lived long enough in the country to see for himself the fearful devastations sometimes wrought by these ravenous insects in their campaigns for food. But since then he had planned measures of defense accordingly, and these, he was convinced? were in every way adequate to withstand the approaching peril.

Moreover, during his three years as a planter, Leiningen had met and defeated drought, Hood, plague and all other "acts of God" which had come against him—unlike his fellow-settlers in the district, who had made little or no resistance. This unbroken success he attributed solely to the observance of his lifelong motto: The human brain needs only to become fully aware of its powers to conquer even the elements. Dullards reeled senselessly and aimlessly into the abyss; cranks, however brilliant, lost their heads when circumstances suddenly altered or accelerated and ran into stone walls, sluggards drifted with the current until they were caught in whirlpools and dragged under. But such disasters, Leiningen contended, merely strengthened his argument that intelligence, directed aright, invariably makes man the master of his fate.

Yes, Leiningen had always known how to grapple with life. Even here, in this Brazilian wilderness, his brain had triumphed over every difficulty and danger it had so far encountered. First he had vanquished primal forces by cunning and organization, then he had enlisted the resources of modern science to increase miraculously the yield of his plantation. And now he was sure he would prove more than a match for the "irresistible" ants.

That same evening, however, Leiningen assembled his workers. He had no intention of waiting till the news reached their ears from other sources. Most of them had been born in the district; the cry "The ants are coming!" was to them an imperative signal for instant, panic-stricken flight, a spring for life itself. But so great was the Indians' trust in Leiningen, in Leiningen's word, and in Leiningen's wisdom, that they received his curt tidings, and his orders for the imminent struggle, with the calmness with which they were given. They waited, unafraid, alert, as if for the beginning of a new game or hunt which he had just described to them. The ants were indeed mighty, but not so mighty as the boss. Let them come!

They came at noon the second day. Their approach was announced by the wild unrest of the horses, scarcely controllable now either in stall or under rider, scenting from afar a vapor instinct with horror.

It was announced by a stampede of animals, timid and savage, hurtling past each other; jaguars and pumas flashing by nimble stags of the pampas, bulky tapirs, no longer hunters, themselves hunted, outpacing fleet kinkajous, maddened herds of cattle, heads lowered, nostrils snorting, rushing through tribes of loping monkeys, chattering in a dementia of terror; then followed the creeping and springing denizens of bush and steppe, big and little rodents, snakes, and lizards.

Pell-mell the rabble swarmed down the hill to the plantation, scattered right and left before the barrier of the water-filled ditch, then sped onwards to the river, where, again hindered, they fled along its bank out of sight.

This water-filled ditch was one of the defense measures which Leiningen had long since prepared against the advent of the ants. It encompassed three sides of the plantation like a huge horseshoe. Twelve feet across, but not very deep, when dry it could hardly be described as an obstacle to either man or beast. But the ends of the "horseshoe" ran into the river which formed the northern boundary, and fourth side, of the plantation. And at the end nearer the house and outbuildings in the middle of the plantation, Leiningen had constructed a dam by means of which water from the river could be diverted into the ditch.

So now, by opening the dam, he was able to fling an imposing girdle of water, a huge quadrilateral with the river as its base, completely around the plantation, like the moat encircling a medieval city. Unless the ants were clever enough to build rafts. They had no hope of reaching the plantation, Leiningen concluded.

The twelve-foot water ditch seemed to afford in itself all the security needed. But while awaiting the arrival of the ants, Leiningen made a further improvement. The western section of the ditch ran along the edge of a tamarind wood, and the branches of some great trees reached over the water. Leiningen now had them lopped so that ants could not descend from them within the "moat."

The women and children, then the herds of cattle, were escorted by peons on rafts over the river, to remain on the other side in absolute safety until the plunderers had departed. Leiningen gave this instruction, not because he believed the noncombatants were in any danger, but in order to avoid hampering the efficiency of the defenders. "Critical situations first become crises," he explained to his men, "when oxen or women get excited."

Finally, he made a careful inspection of the "inner moat"—a smaller ditch lined with concrete, which extended around the hill on which stood the ranch house, barns, stables and other buildings. Into this concrete ditch emptied the inflow pipes from three great petrol tanks. If by some miracle the ants managed to cross the water and reached the plantation, this "rampart of petrol," would be an absolutely impassable protection for the besieged and their dwellings and stock. Such, at least, was Leiningen's opinion.

He stationed his men at irregular distances along the water ditch, the first line of defense. Then he lay down in his hammock and puffed drowsily away at his pipe until a peon came with the report that the ants had been observed far away in the South.

Leiningen mounted his horse, which at the feel of its master seemed to forget its uneasiness, and rode leisurely in the direction of the threatening offensive. The southern stretch of ditch—

the upper side of the quadrilateral—was nearly three miles long; from its center one could survey the entire countryside. This was destined to be the scene of the outbreak of war between Leiningen's brain and twenty square miles of life-destroying ants.

It was a sight one could never forget. Over the range of hills, as far as eye could see, crept a darkening hem, ever longer and broader, until the shadow spread across the slope from east to west, then downwards, downwards, uncannily swift, and all the green herbage of that wide vista was being mown as by a giant sickle, leaving only the vast moving shadow, extending, deepening, and moving rapidly nearer.

When Leiningen's men, behind their barrier of water, perceived the approach of the long-expected foe, they gave vent to their suspense in screams and imprecations. But as the distance began to lessen between the "sons of hell" and the water ditch, they relapsed into silence. Before the advance of that awe-inspiring throng, their belief in the powers of the boss began to steadily dwindle.

Even Leiningen himself, who had ridden up just in time to restore their loss of heart by a display of unshakable calm, even he could not free himself from a qualm of malaise. Yonder were thousands of millions of voracious jaws bearing down upon him and only a suddenly insignificant, narrow ditch lay between him and his men and being gnawed to the bones "before you can spit three times."

Hadn't this brain for once taken on more than it could manage? If the blighters decided to rush the ditch, fill it to the brim with their corpses, there'd still be more than enough to destroy every trace of that cranium of his. The planter's chin jutted; they hadn't got him yet, and he'd see to it they never would. While he could think at all, he'd flout both death and the devil.

The hostile army was approaching in perfect formation; no human battalions, however well-drilled, could ever hope to rival the precision of that advance. Along a front that moved forward as uniformly as a straight line, the ants drew nearer and nearer to the water ditch. Then, when they learned through their scouts the nature of the obstacle, the two outlying wings of the army detached themselves from the main body and marched down the western and eastern sides of the ditch.

This surrounding maneuver took rather more than an hour to accomplish; no doubt the ants expected that at some point they would find a crossing.

During this outflanking movement by the wings, the army on the center and southern front remained still. The besieged were therefore able to contemplate at their leisure the thumb-long, reddish black, long-legged insects; some of the Indians believed they could see, too, intent on them, the brilliant, cold eyes, and the razor-edged mandibles, of this host of infinity.

It is not easy for the average person to imagine that an animal, not to mention an insect, can think. But now both the European brain of Leiningen and the primitive brains of the Indians began to stir with the unpleasant foreboding that inside every single one of that deluge of insects dwelt a thought. And that thought was: Ditch or no ditch, we'll get to your flesh!

Not until four o'clock did the wings reach the "horseshoe" ends of the ditch, only to find these ran into the great river. Through some kind of secret telegraphy, the report must then have flashed very swiftly indeed along the entire enemy line. And Leiningen, riding—no longer casually—along his side of the ditch, noticed by energetic and widespread movements of troops that for some unknown reason the news of the check had its greatest effect on the southern front, where the main army was massed. Perhaps the failure to find a way over the ditch was persuading the ants to withdraw from the plantation in search of spoils more easily attainable.

An immense flood of ants, about a hundred yards in width, was pouring in a glimmering-black cataract down the far slope of the ditch. Many thousands were already drowning in the sluggish creeping flow, but they were followed by troop after troop, who clambered over their sinking comrades, and then themselves served as dying bridges to the reserves hurrying on in their rear.

Shoals of ants were being carried away by the current into the middle of the ditch, where gradually they broke asunder and then, exhausted by their struggles, vanished below the surface. Nevertheless, the wavering, floundering hundred-yard front was remorselessly if slowly advancing towards the besieged on the other bank. Leiningen had been wrong when he supposed the enemy would first have to fill the ditch with their bodies before they could cross; instead, they merely needed to act as stepping-stones, as they swam and sank, to the hordes ever pressing onwards from behind.

Near Leiningen a few mounted herdsmen awaited his orders. He sent one to the weir-the river must be dammed more strongly to increase the speed and power of the water coursing through the ditch.

A second peon was dispatched to the outhouses to bring spades and petrol sprinklers. A third rode away to summon to the zone of the offensive all the men, except the observation posts, on the near-by sections of the ditch, which were not yet actively threatened.

The ants were getting across far more quickly than Leiningen would have deemed possible. Impelled by the mighty cascade behind them, they struggled nearer and nearer to the inner bank. The momentum of the attack was so great that neither the tardy flow of the stream nor its downward pull could exert its proper force; and into the gap left by every submerging insect, hastened forward a dozen more.

When reinforcements reached Leiningen, the invaders were halfway over. The planter had to admit to himself that it was only by a stroke of luck for him that the ants were attempting the crossing on a relatively short front: had they assaulted simultaneously along the entire length of the ditch, the outlook for the defenders would have been black indeed.

Even as it was, it could hardly be described as rosy, though the planter seemed quite unaware that death in a gruesome form was drawing closer and closer. As the war between his brain and the "act of God" reached its climax, the very shadow of annihilation began to pale to Leiningen, who now felt like a champion in a new Olympic game, a gigantic and thrilling contest, from which he was determined to emerge victor. Such, indeed, was his aura of confidence that the Indians forgot their stupefied fear of the peril only a yard or two away; under the planter's supervision, they began fervidly digging up to the edge of the bank and throwing clods of earth and spadefuls of sand into the midst of the hostile fleet.

The petrol sprinklers, hitherto used to destroy pests and

blights on the plantation, were also brought into action. Streams of evil-reeking oil now soared and fell over an enemy already in disorder through the bombardment of earth and sand.

The ants responded to these vigorous and successful measures of defense by further developments of their offensive. Entire clumps of huddling insects began to roll down the opposite bank into the water. At the same time, Leiningen noticed that the ants were now attacking along an ever-widening front. As the numbers both of his men and his petrol sprinklers were severely limited, this rapid extension of the line of battle was becoming an overwhelming danger.

To add to his difficulties, the very clods of earth they flung into that black floating carpet often whirled fragments toward the defenders' side, and here and there dark ribbons were already mounting the inner bank. True, wherever a man saw these they could still be driven back into the water by spadefuls of earth or jets of petrol. But the file of defenders was too sparse and scattered to hold off at all points these landing parties, and though the peons toiled like madmen, their plight became momentarily more perilous.

One man struck with his spade at an enemy clump, did not draw it back quickly enough from the water; in a trice the wooden shaft swarmed with upward scurrying insects. With a curse, he dropped the spade into the ditch; too late, they were already on his body. They lost no time; wherever they encountered bare flesh they bit deeply; a few, bigger than the rest, carried in their hind-quarters a sting which injected a burning and paralyzing venom. Screaming, frantic with pain, the peon danced and twirled like a dervish.

Realizing that another such casualty, yes, perhaps this alone, might plunge his men into confusion and destroy their morale, Leiningen roared in a bellow louder than the yells of the victim: "Into the petrol, idiot! Douse your paws in the petrol!" The dervish ceased his pirouette as if transfixed, then tore of his shirt and plunged his arm and the ants hanging to it up to the shoulder in one of the large open tins of petrol. But even then the fierce mandibles did not slacken; another peon had to help him squash and detach each separate insect.

Distracted by the episode, some defenders had turned away

from the ditch. And now cries of fury, a thudding of spades, and a wild trampling to and fro, showed that the ants had made full use of the interval, though luckily only a few had managed to get across. The men set to work again desperately with the barrage of earth and sand. Meanwhile an old Indian, who acted as medicine-man to the plantation workers, gave the bitten peon a drink he had prepared some hours before, which, he claimed, possessed the virtue of dissolving and weakening ants' venom.

Leiningen surveyed his position. A dispassionate observer would have estimated the odds against him at a thousand to one. But then such an on-looker would have reckoned only by what he saw—the advance of myriad battalions of ants against the futile efforts of a few defenders—and not by the unseen activity that can go on in a man's brain.

For Leiningen had not erred when he decided he would fight elemental with elemental. The water in the ditch was beginning to rise; the stronger damming of the river was making itself apparent.

Visibly the swiftness and power of the masses of water increased, swirling into quicker and quicker movement its living black surface, dispersing its pattern, carrying away more and more of it on the hastening current.

Victory had been snatched from the very jaws of defeat. With a hysterical shout of joy, the peons feverishly intensified their bombardment of earth clods and sand.

And now the wide cataract down the opposite bank was thinning and ceasing, as if the ants were becoming aware that they could not attain their aim. They were scurrying back up the slope to safety.

All the troops so far hurled into the ditch had been sacrificed in vain. Drowned and floundering insects eddied in thousands along the flow, while Indians running on the bank destroyed every swimmer that reached the side.

Not until the ditch curved towards the east did the scattered ranks assemble again in a coherent mass. And now, exhausted and half-numbed, they were in no condition to ascend the bank. Fusillades of clods drove them round the bend towards the mouth of the ditch and then into the river, wherein they vanished without leaving a trace.

The news ran swiftly along the entire chain of outposts, and soon a long scattered line of laughing men could be seen hastening along the ditch towards the scene of victory.

For once they seemed to have lost all their native reserve, for it was in wild abandon now they celebrated the triumph—as if there were no longer thousands of millions of merciless, cold and hungry eyes watching them from the opposite bank, watching and waiting.

The sun sank behind the rim of the tamarind wood and twilight deepened into night. It was not only hoped but expected that the ants would remain quiet until dawn. "But to defeat any forlorn attempt at a crossing, the flow of water through the ditch was powerfully increased by opening the dam still further.

In spite of this impregnable barrier, Leiningen was not yet altogether convinced that the ants would not venture another surprise attack. He ordered his men to camp along the bank overnight. He also detailed parties of them to patrol the ditch in two of his motor cars and ceaselessly to illuminate the surface of the water with headlights and electric torches.

After having taken all the precautions he deemed necessary, the farmer ate his supper with considerable appetite and went to bed. His slumbers were in no wise disturbed by the memory of the waiting, live, twenty square miles.

Dawn found a thoroughly refreshed and active Leiningen riding along the edge of the ditch. The planter saw before him a motionless and unaltered throng of besiegers. He studied the wide belt of water between them and the plantation, and for a moment almost regretted that the fight had ended so soon and so simply. In the comforting, matter-of-fact light of morning, it seemed to him now that the ants hadn't the ghost of a chance to cross the ditch. Even if they plunged headlong into it on all three fronts at once, the force of the now powerful current would inevitably sweep them away. He had got quite a thrill out of the fight—a pity it was already over.

He rode along the eastern and southern sections of the ditch and found everything in order. He reached the western section, opposite the tamarind wood, and here, contrary to the other battle fronts, he found the enemy very busy indeed. The trunks and branches of the trees and the creepers of the lianas, on the far bank of the ditch, fairly swarmed with industrious insects. But instead of eating the leaves there and then, they were merely gnawing through the stalks, so that a thick green shower fell steadily to the ground.

No doubt they were victualing columns sent out to obtain provender for the rest of the army. The discovery did not surprise Leiningen. He did not need to be told that ants are intelligent, that certain species even use others as milch cows, watchdogs and slaves. He was well aware of their power of adaptation, their sense of discipline, their marvelous talent for organization.

His belief that a foray to supply the army was in progress was strengthened when he saw the leaves that fell to the ground being dragged to the troops waiting outside the wood. Then all at once he realized the aim that rain of green was intended to serve.

Each single leaf, pulled or pushed by dozens of toiling insects, was borne straight to the edge of the ditch. Even as Macbeth watched the approach of Birnam Wood in the hands of his enemies, Leiningen saw the tamarind wood move nearer and nearer in the mandibles of the ants. Unlike the fey Scot, however, he did not lose his nerve; no witches had prophesied his doom, and if they had he would have slept just as soundly. All the same, he was forced to admit to himself that the situation was far more ominous than that of the day before.

He had thought it impossible for the ants to build rafts for themselves—well, here they were, coming in thousands, more than enough to bridge the ditch. Leaves after leaves rustled down the slope into the water, where the current drew them away from the bank and carried them into midstream. And every single leaf carried several ants. This time the farmer did not trust to the alacrity of his messengers. He galloped away, leaning from his saddle and yelling orders as he rushed past outpost after outpost: “Bring petrol pumps to the southwest front! Issue spades to every man along the line facing the wood!” And arrived at the eastern and southern sections, he dispatched every man except the observation posts to the menaced west.

Then, as he rode past the stretch where the ants had failed to cross the day before, he witnessed a brief but impressive scene. Down the slope of the distant hill there came towards him a singular being, writhing rather man running, an animal-like blackened statue with shapeless head and four quivering feet that knuckled under almost ceaselessly. When the creature reached the far bank of the ditch and collapsed opposite Leiningen, he recognized it as a pampas stag, covered over and over with ants.

It had strayed near the zone of the army. As usual, they had attacked its eyes first. Blinded, it had reeled in the madness of hideous torment straight into the ranks of its persecutors, and now the beast swayed to and fro in its death agony.

With a shot from his rifle Leiningen put it out of its misery. Then he pulled out his watch. He hadn't a second to lose, but for life itself he could not have denied his curiosity the satisfaction of knowing how long the ants would take—for personal reasons, so to speak. After six minutes the white polished bones alone remained. That's how he himself would look before you can—Leiningen spat once, and put spurs to his horse.

The sporting zest with which the excitement of the novel contest had inspired him the day before had now vanished; in its place was a cold and violent purpose. He would send these vermin back to the hell where they belonged, somehow, anyhow. Yes, but how was indeed the question; as things stood at present it looked as if the devils would raze him and his men from the earth instead. He had underestimated the might of the enemy; he really would have to bestir himself if he hoped to outwit them.

The biggest danger now, he decided, was the point where the western section of the ditch curved southwards. And arrived there, he found his worst expectations justified. The very power of the current had huddled the leaves and their crews of ants so close together at the bend that the bridge was almost ready.

True, streams of petrol and clumps of earth still prevented a landing. But the number of floating leaves was increasing ever more swiftly. It could not be long now before a stretch of water a mile in length was decked by a green pontoon over which the ants could rush in millions.

Leiningen galloped to the weir. The damming of the river was controlled by a wheel on its bank. The planter ordered the man at the wheel first to lower the water in the ditch almost to vanishing point, next to wait a moment, then suddenly to let the river in again. This maneuver of lowering and raising the surface, of decreasing then increasing the flow of water through the ditch was to be repeated over and over again until further notice.

This tactic was at first successful. The water in the ditch sank, and with it the film of leaves. The green fleet nearly reached the bed and the troops on the far bank swarmed down the slope to it. Then a violent flow of water at the original depth raced through the ditch, overwhelming leaves and ants, and sweeping them along.

This intermittent rapid flushing prevented just in time the almost completed fording of the ditch. But it also flung here and there squads of the enemy vanguard simultaneously up the inner bank. These seemed to know their duty only too well, and lost no time accomplishing it. The air rang with the curses of bitten Indians. They had removed their shirts and pants to detect the quicker the upwards-hastening insects; when they saw one, they crushed it; and fortunately the onslaught as yet was only by skirmishers. Again and again, the water sank and rose, carrying leaves and drowned ants away with it. It lowered once more nearly to its bed; but this time the exhausted defenders waited in vain for the flush of destruction. Leiningen sensed disaster; something must have gone wrong with the machinery of the dam. Then a sweating peon tore up to him—

"They're over!"

While the besieged were concentrating upon the defense of the stretch opposite the wood, the seemingly unaffected line beyond the wood had become the theatre of decisive action. Here the defenders' front was sparse and scattered; everyone who could be spared had hurried away to the south.

Just as the man at the weir had lowered the water almost to the bed of the ditch, the ants on a wide front began another attempt at a direct crossing like that of the preceding day. Into the emptied bed poured an irresistible throng. Rushing across the ditch, they attained the inner bank before the slow-witted Indians fully grasped the situation. Their frantic screams dumfounded the man at the weir. Before he could direct the river anew into the safeguarding bed he saw himself surrounded by raging ants. He ran like the others, ran for his life.

When Leiningen heard this, he knew the plantation was

doomed. He wasted no time bemoaning the inevitable. For as long as there was the slightest chance of success, he had stood his ground, and now any further resistance was both useless and dangerous. He fired three revolver shots into the air—the prearranged signal for his men to retreat instantly within the "inner moat." Then he rode towards the ranch house.

This was two miles from the point of invasion. There was therefore time enough to prepare the second line of defense against the advent of the ants. Of the three great petrol cisterns near the house, one had already been half emptied by the constant withdrawals needed for the pumps during the fight at the water ditch. The remaining petrol in it was now drawn off through underground pipes into the concrete trench which encircled the ranch house and its outbuildings.

And there, drifting in twos and threes, Leiningen's men reached him. Most of them were obviously trying to preserve an air of calm and indifference, belied, however, by their restless glances and knitted brows. One could see their belief in a favorable outcome of the struggle was already considerably shaken.

The planter called his peons around him.

"Well, lads," he began, "we've lost the first round. But we'll smash the beggars yet, don't you worry. Anyone who thinks otherwise can draw his pay here and now and push off. There are rafts enough to spare on the river and plenty of time still to reach 'em."

Not a man stirred.

Leiningen acknowledged his silent vote of confidence with a laugh that was half a grunt. "That's the stuff, lads. Too bad if you'd missed the rest of the show, eh? Well, the fun won't start till morning. Once these blighters turn tail, there'll be plenty of work for everyone and higher wages all round. And now run along and get something to eat; you've earned it all right."

In the excitement of the fight the greater part of the day had passed without the men once pausing to snatch a bite. Now that the ants were for the time being out of sight, and the "wall of petrol" gave a stronger feeling of security, hungry stomachs began to assert their claims.

The bridges over the concrete ditch were removed. Here and there solitary ants had reached the ditch; they gazed at the petrol meditatively, then scurried back again. Apparently they had little interest at the moment for what lay beyond the evil-reeking barrier; the abundant spoils of the plantation were the main attraction. Soon the trees, shrubs and beds for miles around were hulled with ants zealously gobbling the yield of long weary months of strenuous toil.

As twilight began to fall, a cordon of ants marched around the petrol trench, but as yet made no move towards its brink. Leiningen posted sentries with headlights and electric torches, then withdrew to his office, and began to reckon up his losses. He estimated these as large, but, in comparison with his bank balance, by no means unbearable. He worked out in some detail a scheme of intensive cultivation which would enable him, before very long, to more than compensate himself for the damage now being wrought to his crops. It was with a contented mind that he finally betook himself to bed where he slept deeply until dawn, undisturbed by any thought that next day little more might be left of him than a glistening skeleton.

He rose with the sun and went out on the flat roof of his house. And a scene like one from Dante lay around him; for miles in every direction there was nothing but a black, glittering multitude, a multitude of rested, sated, but none the less voracious ants: yes, look as far as one might, one could see nothing but that rustling black throng, except in the north, where the great river drew a boundary they could not hope to pass. But even the high stone breakwater, along the bank of the river, which Leiningen had built as a defense against inundations, was, like the paths, the shorn trees and shrubs, the ground itself, black with ants.

So their greed was not glutted in razing that vast plantation? Not by a long shot; they were all the more eager now on a rich and certain booty—four hundred men, numerous horses, and bursting granaries.

At first it seemed that the petrol trench would serve its purpose. The besiegers sensed the peril of swimming it, and made no move to plunge blindly over its brink. Instead they devised a better maneuver; they began to collect shreds of bark, twigs and dried leaves and dropped these into the petrol. Everything green, which could have been similarly used, had long since been eaten.

After a time, though, a long procession could be seen bringing from the west the tamarind leaves used as rafts the day before.

Since the petrol, unlike the water in the outer ditch, was perfectly still, the refuse stayed where it was thrown. It was several hours before the ants succeeded in covering an appreciable part of the surface. At length, however, they were ready to proceed to a direct attack.

Their storm troops swarmed down the concrete side, scrambled over the supporting surface of twigs and leaves, and impelled these over the few remaining streaks of open petrol until they reached the other side. Then they began to climb up this to make straight for the helpless garrison.

During the entire offensive, the planter sat peacefully, watching them with interest, but not stirring a muscle. Moreover, he had ordered his men not to disturb in any way whatever the advancing horde. So they squatted listlessly along the bank of the ditch and waited for a sign from the boss. The petrol was now covered with ants. A few had climbed the inner concrete wall and were scurrying towards the defenders.

"Everyone back from the ditch!" roared Leiningen. The men rushed away, without the slightest idea of his plan. He stooped forward and cautiously dropped into the ditch a stone which split the floating carpet and its living freight, to reveal a gleaming patch of petrol. A match spurted, sank down to the oily surface—Leiningen sprang back; in a flash a towering rampart of fire encompassed the garrison.

This spectacular and instant repulse threw the Indians into ecstasy. They applauded, yelled and stamped, like children at a pantomime. Had it not been for the awe in which they held the boss, they would infallibly have carried him shoulder high.

It was some time before the petrol burned down to the bed of the ditch, and the wall of smoke and flame began to lower. The ants had retreated in a wide circle from the devastation, and innumerable charred fragments along the outer bank showed that the flames had spread from the holocaust in the ditch well into the ranks beyond, where they had wrought havoc far and wide.

Yet the perseverance of the ants was by no means broken; indeed, each setback seemed only to whet it. The concrete cooled, the flicker of the dying flames wavered and vanished, petrol from the second tank poured into the trench—and the ants marched forward anew to the attack.

The foregoing scene repeated itself in every detail, except that on this occasion less time was needed to bridge the ditch, for the petrol was now already filmed by a layer of ash. Once again they withdrew; once again petrol flowed into the ditch. Would the creatures never learn that their self-sacrifice was utterly senseless? It really was senseless, wasn't it? Yes, of course it was senseless—provided the defenders had an unlimited supply of petrol.

When Leiningen reached this stage of reasoning, he felt for the first time since the arrival of the ants that his confidence was deserting him. His skin began to creep; he loosened his collar. Once the devils were over the trench there wasn't a chance in hell for him and his men. God, what a prospect, to be eaten alive like that!

For the third time the flames immolated the attacking troops, and burned down to extinction. Yet the ants were coming on again as if nothing had happened. And meanwhile Leiningen had made a discovery that chilled him to the bone-petrol was no longer flowing into the ditch. Something must be blocking the outflow pipe of the third and last cistern-a snake or a dead rat? Whatever it was, the ants could be held off no longer, unless petrol could by some method be led from the cistern into the ditch.

Then Leiningen remembered that in an outhouse nearby were two old disused fire engines. Spry as never before in their lives, the peons dragged them out of the shed, connected their pumps to the cistern, uncoiled and laid the hose. They were just in time to aim a stream of petrol at a column of ants that had already crossed and drive them back down the incline into the ditch. Once more an oily girdle surrounded the garrison, once more it was possible to hold the position—for the moment.

It was obvious, however, that this last resource meant only the postponement of defeat and death. A few of the peons fell on their knees and began to pray; others, shrieking insanely, fired their revolvers at the black, advancing masses, as if they felt their despair was pitiful enough to sway fate itself to mercy.

At length, two of the men's nerves broke: Leiningen saw a naked Indian leap over the north side of the petrol trench, quickly followed by a second. They sprinted with incredible speed towards the river. But their fleetness did not save them; long before they could attain the rafts, the enemy covered their bodies from head to foot.

In the agony of their torment, both sprang blindly into the wide river, where enemies no less sinister awaited them. Wild screams of mortal anguish informed the breathless onlookers that crocodiles and sword-toothed piranhas were no less ravenous than ants, and even nimbler in reaching their prey.

In spite of this bloody warning, more and more men showed they were making up their minds to run the blockade. Anything, even a fight midstream against alligators, seemed better than powerlessly waiting for death to come and slowly consume their living bodies.

Leiningen flogged his brain till it reeled. Was there nothing on earth could sweep this devil's spawn back into the hell from which it came?

Then out of the inferno of his bewilderment rose a terrifying inspiration. Yes, one hope remained, and one alone. It might be possible to dam the great river completely, so that its waters would fill not only the water ditch but overflow into the entire gigantic "saucer" of land in which lay the plantation.

The far bank of the river was too high for the waters to escape that way. The stone breakwater ran between the river and the plantation; its only gaps occurred where the "horseshoe" ends of the water ditch passed into the river. So its waters would not only be forced to inundate into the plantation, they would also be held there by the breakwater until they rose to its own high level. In half an hour, perhaps even earlier, the plantation and its hostile army of occupation would be flooded.

The ranch house and outbuildings stood upon rising ground. Their foundations were higher than the breakwater, so the flood would not reach them. And any remaining ants trying to ascend the slope could be repulsed by petrol.

It was possible—yes, if one could only get to the dam! A distance of nearly two miles lay between the ranch house and the weir—two miles of ants. Those two peons had managed only a fifth of that distance at the cost of their lives. Was there an Indian daring enough after that to run the gauntlet five times as far? Hardly likely; and if there were, his prospect of getting back was almost nil.

No, there was only one thing for it, he'd have to make the attempt himself; he might just as well be running as sitting still, anyway, when the ants finally got him. Besides, there was a bit of a chance. Perhaps the ants weren't so almighty, after all; perhaps he had allowed the mass suggestion of that evil black throng to hypnotize him, just as a snake fascinates and overpowers.

The ants were building their bridges. Leiningen got up on a chair. "Hey, lads, listen to me!" he cried. Slowly and listlessly, from all sides of the trench, the men began to shuffle towards him, the apathy of death already stamped on their faces.

"Listen, lads!" he shouted. "You're frightened of those beggars, but you're a damn sight more frightened of me, and I'm proud of you. There's still a chance to save our lives—by flooding the plantation from the river. Now one of you might manage to get as far as the weir—but he'd never come back. Well, I'm not going to let you try it; if I did I'd be worse than one of those ants. No, I called the tune, and now I'm going to pay the piper.

"The moment I'm over the ditch, set fire to the petrol. That'll allow time for the flood to do the trick. Then all you have to do is wait here all snug and quiet till I'm back. Yes, I'm coming back, trust me"—he grinned—"when I've finished my slimming-cure."

He pulled on high leather boots, drew heavy gauntlets over his hands, and stuffed the spaces between breeches and boots, gauntlets and arms, shirt and neck, with rags soaked in petrol. With close-fitting mosquito goggles he shielded his eyes, knowing too well the ants' dodge of first robbing their victim of sight. Finally, he plugged his nostrils and ears with cotton-wool, and let the peons drench his clothes with petrol.

He was about to set off, when the old Indian medicine man came up to him; he had a wondrous salve, he said, prepared from a species of chafer whose odor was intolerable to ants. Yes, this odor protected these chafers from the attacks of even the most murderous ants. The Indian smeared the boss' boots, his gauntlets, and his face over and over with the extract.

Leiningen then remembered the paralyzing effect of ants'

venom, and the Indian gave him a gourd full of the medicine he had administered to the bitten peon at the water ditch. The planter drank it down without noticing its bitter taste; his mind was already at the weir.

He started of towards the northwest corner of the trench. With a bound he was over—and among the ants.

The beleaguered garrison had no opportunity to watch Leiningen's race against death. The ants were climbing the inner bank again-the lurid ring of petrol blazed aloft. For the fourth time that day the reflection from the fire shone on the sweating faces of the imprisoned men, and on the reddish-black cuirasses of their oppressors. The red and blue, dark-edged flames leaped vividly now, celebrating what? The funeral pyre of the four hundred, or of the hosts of destruction? Leiningen ran. He ran in long, equal strides, with only one thought, one sensation, in his being—he must get through. He dodged all trees and shrubs; except for the split seconds his soles touched the ground the ants should have no opportunity to alight on him. That they would get to him soon, despite the salve on his boots, the petrol in his clothes, he realized only too well, but he knew even more surely that he must, and that he would, get to the weir.

Apparently the salve was some use after all; not until he reached halfway did he feel ants under his clothes, and a few on his face. Mechanically, in his stride, he struck at them, scarcely conscious of their bites. He saw he was drawing appreciably nearer the weir—the distance grew less and less—sank to five hundred—three—two—one hundred yards.

Then he was at the weir and gripping the ant-hulled wheel. Hardly had he seized it when a horde of infuriated ants flowed over his hands, arms and shoulders. He started the wheel—before it turned once on its axis the swarm covered his face. Leiningen strained like a madman, his lips pressed tight; if he opened them to draw breath. . . .

He turned and turned; slowly the dam lowered until it reached the bed of the river. Already the water was overflowing the ditch. Another minute, and the river was pouring through the near-by gap in the breakwater. The flooding of the plantation had begun.

Leiningen let go the wheel. Now, for the first time, he realized he was coated from head to foot with a layer of ants. In spite of the petrol his clothes were full of them, several had got to his body or were clinging to his face. Now that he had completed his task, he felt the smart raging over his flesh from the bites of sawing and piercing insects.

Frantic with pain, he almost plunged into the river. To be ripped and splashed to shreds by piranhas? Already he was running the return journey, knocking ants from his gloves and jacket, brushing them from his bloodied face, squashing them to death under his clothes.

One of the creatures bit him just below the rim of his goggles; he managed to tear it away, but the agony of the bite and its etching acid drilled into the eye nerves; he saw now through circles of fire into a milky mist, then he ran for a time almost blinded, knowing that if he once tripped and fell. . . . The old Indian's brew didn't seem much good; it weakened the poison a bit, but didn't get rid of it. His heart pounded as if it would burst; blood roared in his ears; a giant's fist battered his lungs.

Then he could see again, but the burning girdle of petrol appeared infinitely far away; he could not last half that distance. Swift-changing pictures flashed through his head, episodes in his life, while in another part of his brain a cool and impartial onlooker informed this ant-blurred, gasping, exhausted bundle named Leiningen that such a rushing panorama of scenes from one's past is seen only in the moment before death.

A stone in the path . . . to weak to avoid it . . . the planter stumbled and collapsed. He tried to rise . . . he must be pinned under a rock . . . it was impossible . . . the slightest movement was impossible. . . .

Then all at once he saw, starkly clear and huge, and, right before his eyes, furred with ants, towering and swaying in its death agony, the pampas stag. In six minutes—gnawed to the bones. God, he couldn't die like that! And something outside him seemed to drag him to his feet. He tottered. He began to stagger forward again.

Through the blazing ring hurtled an apparition which, as soon as it reached the ground on the inner side, fell full length and did not move. Leiningen, at the moment he made that leap through the flames, lost consciousness for the first time in his life. As he lay there, with glazing eyes and lacerated face, he appeared a man returned from the grave. The peons rushed to him, stripped off his clothes, tore away the ants from a body that seemed almost one open wound; in some places the bones were showing. They carried him into the ranch house.

As the curtain of flames lowered, one could see in place of the illimitable host of ants an extensive vista of water. The thwarted river had swept over the plantation, carrying with it the entire army. The water had collected and mounted in the great "saucer," while the ants had in vain attempted to reach the hill on which stood the ranch house. The girdle of flames held them back.

And so imprisoned between water and fire, they had been delivered into the annihilation that was their god. And near the farther mouth of the water ditch, where the stone mole had its second gap, the ocean swept the lost battalions into the river, to vanish forever.

The ring of fire dwindled as the water mounted to the petrol trench, and quenched the dimming flames. The inundation rose higher and higher: because its outflow was impeded by the timber and underbrush it had carried along with it, its surface required some time to reach the top of the high stone breakwater and discharge over it the rest of the shattered army.

It swelled over ant-stippled shrubs and bushes, until it washed against the foot of the knoll whereon the besieged had taken refuge. For a while an alluvial of ants tried again and again to attain this dry land, only to be repulsed by streams of petrol back into the merciless flood.

Leiningen lay on his bed, his body swathed from head to foot in bandages. With fomentations and salves, they had managed to stop the bleeding, and had dressed his many wounds. Now they thronged around him, one question in every face. Would he recover? "He won't die," said the old man who had bandaged him, "if he doesn't want to."

The planter opened his eyes. "Everything in order?" he asked.

"They're gone," said his nurse. "To hell." He held out to his master a gourd full of a powerful sleeping draught. Leiningen gulped it down.

“I told you I’d come back,” he murmured, “even if I am a bit streamlined.” He grinned and shut his eyes. He slept.

Sredni Vashtar

H. H. Munro (Saki)

Conradin was ten years old, and the doctor had pronounced his professional opinion that the boy would not live another five years. The doctor was silky and effete, and counted for little, but his opinion was endorsed by Mrs. De Ropp, who counted for nearly everything. Mrs. De Ropp was Conradin's cousin and guardian, and in his eyes she represented those three-fifths of the world that are necessary and disagreeable and real; the other two-fifths, in perpetual antagonism to the foregoing, were summed up in himself and his imagination. One of these days Conradin supposed he would succumb to the mastering pressure of wearisome necessary things—such as illnesses and coddling restrictions and drawn-out dullness. Without his imagination, which was rampant under the spur of loneliness, he would have succumbed long ago.

Mrs. De Ropp would never, in her honestest moments, have confessed to herself that she disliked Conradin, though she might have been dimly aware that thwarting him "for his good" was a duty which she did not find particularly irksome. Conradin hated her with a desperate sincerity which he was perfectly able to mask. Such few pleasures as he could contrive for himself gained an added relish from the likelihood that they would be displeasing to his guardian, and from the realm of his imagination she was locked out—an unclean thing, which should find no entrance.

In the dull, cheerless garden, overlooked by so many windows that were ready to open with a message not to do this or that, or a reminder that medicines were due, he found little attraction. The few fruit-trees that it contained were set jealously apart from his plucking, as though they were rare specimens of their kind blooming in an arid waste; it would probably have been difficult to find a market-gardener who would have offered ten shillings for their entire yearly produce. In a forgotten corner, however, almost hidden behind a dismal shrubbery, was a disused tool-shed of respectable proportions, and within its walls Conradin found a haven, something that took on the varying aspects of a playroom and a cathedral. He had peopled it with a legion of familiar phantoms, evoked partly from fragments of history and partly from his own brain, but it also boasted two inmates of flesh and blood. In one corner lived a ragged-plumaged Houdan hen, on which the boy lavished an affection that had scarcely another outlet. Further back in the gloom stood a large hutch, divided into two compartments, one of which was fronted with close iron bars. This was the abode of a large polecat-ferret, which a friendly butcher-boy had once smuggled, cage and all, into its present quarters, in exchange for a long-secreted hoard of small silver. Conradin was dreadfully afraid of the lithe, sharp-fanged beast, but it was his most treasured possession. Its very presence in the tool-shed was a secret and fearful joy, to be kept scrupulously from the knowledge of the Woman, as he privately dubbed his cousin. And one day, out of Heaven knows what material, he spun the beast a wonderful name, and from that moment it grew into a god and a religion. The Woman indulged in religion once a week at a church near by, and took Conradin with her, but to him the church service was an alien rite in the House of Rimmon. Every Thursday, in the dim and musty silence of the tool-shed, he worshipped with mystic and elaborate ceremonial before the wooden hutch where dwelt Sredni Vashtar, the great ferret. Red flowers in their season and scarlet berries in the winter-time were offered at his shrine, for he was a god who laid some special stress on the fierce impatient side of things, as opposed to the Woman's religion, which, as far as Conradin could observe, went to great lengths in the contrary direction. And on great festivals powdered nutmeg was strewn in front of his hutch, an important feature of the offering being that the nutmeg had to be stolen. These festivals were of irregular occurrence, and were chiefly appointed to celebrate some passing event. On one occasion, when Mrs. De Ropp suffered from acute toothache for three days, Conradin kept up the festival during the entire three days, and almost succeeded in persuading himself that Sredni Vashtar was personally responsible for the toothache. If the malady had lasted for another day the supply of nutmeg would have given out.

The Houdan hen was never drawn into the cult of Sredni Vashtar. Conradin had long ago settled that she was an Anabaptist. He did not pretend to have the remotest knowledge as to what an Anabaptist was, but he privately hoped that it was dashing and not very respectable. Mrs. De Ropp was the ground plan on which he based and detested all respectability.

After a while Conradin's absorption in the tool-shed began to attract the notice of his guardian. "It is not good for him to be pottering down there in all weathers," she promptly decided, and at breakfast one morning she announced that the Houdan hen had been sold and taken away overnight. With her shortsighted eyes she peered at Conradin, waiting for an outbreak of rage and sorrow, which she was ready to rebuke with a flow of excellent precepts and reasoning. But Conradin said nothing: there was nothing to be said. Something perhaps in his white set face gave her a momentary qualm, for at tea that afternoon there was toast on the table, a delicacy which she usually banned on the ground that it was bad for him; also because the making of it "gave trouble," a deadly offence in the middle-class feminine eye.

"I thought you liked toast," she exclaimed, with an injured air, observing that he did not touch it.

"Sometimes," said Conradin.

In the shed that evening there was an innovation in the worship of the hutch-god. Conradin had been wont to chant his praises, tonight he asked a boon.

"Do one thing for me, Sredni Vashtar."

The thing was not specified. As Sredni Vashtar was a god he must be supposed to know. And choking back a sob as he looked at that other empty comer, Conradin went back to the world he so hated.

And every night, in the welcome darkness of his bedroom, and every evening in the dusk of the tool-shed, Conradin's bitter litany went up: "Do one thing for me, Sredni Vashtar."

Mrs. De Ropp noticed that the visits to the shed did not cease, and one day she made a further journey of inspection.

"What are you keeping in that locked hutch?" she asked. "I believe it's guinea-pigs. I'll have them all cleared away."

Conradin shut his lips tight, but the Woman ransacked his bedroom till she found the carefully hidden key, and forthwith marched down to the shed to complete her discovery. It was a cold afternoon, and Conradin had been bidden to keep to the house. From the furthest window of the dining-room the door of the shed could just be seen beyond the corner of the shrubbery, and there Conradin stationed himself. He saw the Woman enter, and then he imagined her opening the door of the sacred hutch and peering down with her short-sighted eyes into the thick straw bed where his god lay hidden. Perhaps she would prod at the straw in her clumsy impatience. And Conradin fervently breathed his prayer for the last time. But he knew as he prayed that he did not believe. He knew that the Woman would come out presently with that pursed smile he loathed so well on her face, and that in an hour or two the gardener would carry away his wonderful god, a god no longer, but a simple brown ferret in a hutch. And he knew that the Woman would triumph always as she triumphed now, and that he would grow ever more sickly under her pestering and domineering and superior wisdom, till one day nothing would matter much more with him, and the doctor would be proved right. And in the sting and misery of his defeat, he began to chant loudly and defiantly the hymn of his threatened idol:

Sredni Vashtar went forth,
His thoughts were red thought and his teeth were white.
His enemies called for peace, but he brought them death.
Sredni Vashtar the Beautiful.

And then of a sudden he stopped his chanting and drew closer to the window-pane. The door of the shed still stood ajar as it had been left, and the minutes were slipping by. They were long minutes, but they slipped by nevertheless. He watched the starlings running and flying in little parties across the lawn; he counted them over and over again, with one eye always on that swinging door. A sour-faced maid came in to lay the table for tea, and still Conradin stood and waited and watched. Hope had crept by inches into his heart, and now a look of triumph began to blaze in his eyes that had only known the wistful patience of defeat. Under his breath, with a furtive exultation, he began once again the pæan of victory and devastation. And presently his eyes were rewarded: out through that doorway came a long, low, yellow-and-brown beast, with eyes a-blink at the waning daylight, and dark wet stains around the fur of jaws and throat. Conradin dropped on his knees. The great polecat-ferret made its way down to a small brook at the foot of the garden, drank for a moment, then crossed a little plank bridge and was lost to sight in the bushes. Such was the passing of Sredni Vashtar.

"Tea is ready," said the sour-faced maid; "where is the mistress?" "She went down to the shed some time ago," said Conradin. And while the maid went to summon her mistress to tea, Conradin fished a toasting-fork out of the sideboard drawer and proceeded to toast himself a piece of bread. And during the toasting of it and the buttering of it with much butter and the slow enjoyment of eating it, Conradin listened to the noises and silences which fell in quick spasms beyond the dining-room door. The loud foolish screaming of the maid, the answering chorus of wondering ejaculations from the kitchen region, the scuttering footsteps and hurried embassies for outside help, and then, after a lull, the scared sobbings and the shuffling tread of those who bore a heavy burden into the house.

"Whoever will break it to the poor child? I couldn't for the life of me!" exclaimed a shrill voice. And while they debated the matter among themselves, Conradin made himself another piece of toast.

The Killers

Ernest Hemingway

[*Publisher's note: The original Hemingway story contained some racial epithets that were common in his time but extremely offensive in ours; we have altered these.*]

The door of Henry's lunchroom opened and two men came in. They sat down at the counter.

"What's yours?" George asked them.

"I don't know," one of the men said. "What do you want to eat, Al?"

"I don't know," said Al. "I don't know what I want to eat."

Outside it was getting dark. The streetlight came on outside the window. The two men at the counter read the menu. From the other end of the counter Nick Adams watched them. He had been talking to George when they came in.

"I'll have a roast pork tenderloin with apple sauce and mashed potatoes," the first man said.

"It isn't ready yet."

"What the hell do you put it on the card for?"

"That's the dinner," George explained. "You can get that at six o'clock."

George looked at the clock on the wall behind the counter.

"It's five o'clock."

"The clock says twenty minutes past five," the second man said.

"It's twenty minutes fast."

"Oh, to hell with the clock," the first man said. "What have you got to eat?"

"I can give you any kind of sandwiches," George said. "You

can have ham and eggs, bacon and eggs, liver and bacon, or a steak."

"Give me chicken croquettes with green peas and cream sauce and mashed potatoes."

"That's the dinner."

"Everything we want's the dinner, eh? That's the way you work it."

"I can give you ham and eggs, bacon and eggs, liver—"

"I'll take ham and eggs," the man called Al said. He wore a derby hat and a black overcoat buttoned across the chest. His face was small and white and he had tight lips. He wore a silk muffler and gloves.

"Give me bacon and eggs," said the other man. He was about the same size as Al. Their faces were different, but they were dressed like twins. Both wore overcoats too tight for them. They sat leaning forward, their elbows on the counter.

"Got anything to drink?" Al asked.

"Silver beer, bevo, ginger-ale," George said.

"I mean you got anything to drink?"

"Just those I said."

"This is a hot town," said the other. "What do they call it?"

"Summit."

"Ever hear of it?" Al asked his friend.

"No," said the friend.

"What do they do here nights?" Al asked.

"They eat the dinner," his friend said. "They all come here and eat the big dinner."

"That's right," George said.

"So you think that's right?" Al asked George.

"Sure."

"You're a pretty bright boy, aren't you?"

"Sure," said George.

"Well, you're not," said the other little man. "Is he, Al?"

"He's dumb," said Al. He turned to Nick. "What's your name?"

"Adams."

"Another bright boy," Al said. "Ain't he a bright boy, Max?"

"The town's full of bright boys," Max said.

George put the two platters, one of ham and eggs, the other

of bacon and eggs, on the counter. He set down two side dishes of fried potatoes and closed the wicket into the kitchen.

"Which is yours?" he asked Al.

"Don't you remember?"

"Ham and eggs."

"Just a bright boy," Max said. He leaned forward and took the ham and eggs. Both men ate with their gloves on. George watched them eat.

"What are *you* looking at?" Max looked at George.

"Nothing."

"The hell you were. You were looking at me."

"Maybe the boy meant it for a joke, Max," Al said.

George laughed.

"*You* don't have to laugh," Max said to him. "You don't have to laugh at all, see?'

"All right," said George.

"So he thinks it's all right." Max turned to Al. "He thinks it's all right. That's a good one."

"Oh, he's a thinker," Al said. They went on eating.

"What's the bright boy's name down the counter?" Al asked Max.

"Hey, bright boy," Max said to Nick. "You go around on the other side of the counter with your boy friend."

"What's the idea?" Nick asked.

"There isn't any idea."

"You better go around, bright boy," Al said. Nick went around behind the counter.

"What's the idea?" George asked.

"None of your damned business," Al said. "Who's out in the kitchen?"

"The black."

"What do you mean the black?"

"The black that cooks."

"Tell him to come in."

"What's the idea?"

"Tell him to come in."

"Where do you think you are?"

"We know damn well where we are," the man called Max said. "Do we look silly?"

"You talk silly," Al said to him. "What the hell do you argue with this kid for? Listen," he said to George, "tell the black to come out here."

"What are you going to do to him?"

"Nothing. Use your head, bright boy. What would we do to a black?"

George opened the slit that opened back into the kitchen. "Sam," he called. "Come in here a minute."

The door to the kitchen opened and the cook came in. "What was it?" he asked. The two men at the counter took a look at him.

"All right, cook. You stand right there," Al said.

Sam, the black cook, standing in his apron, looked at the two men sitting at the counter. "Yes, sir," he said. Al got down from his stool.

"I'm going back to the kitchen with the black and bright boy," he said. "Go on back to the kitchen, cook. You go with him, bright boy." The little man walked after Nick and Sam, the cook, back into the kitchen. The door shut after them. The man called Max sat at the counter opposite George. He didn't look at George but looked in the mirror that ran along back of the counter. Henry's had been made over from a saloon into a lunch counter.

"Well, bright boy," Max said, looking into the mirror, "why don't you say something?"

"What's it all about?"

"Hey, Al," Max called, "bright boy wants to know what it's all about."

"Why don't you tell him?" Al's voice came from the kitchen.

"What do you think it's all about?"

"I don't know."

"What do you think?"

Max looked into the mirror all the time he was talking.

"I wouldn't say."

"Hey, Al, bright boy says he wouldn't say what he thinks it's all about."

"I can hear you, all right," Al said from the kitchen. He had propped open the slit that dishes passed through into the kitchen with a catsup bottle. "Listen, bright boy," he said from the kitchen to George. "Stand a little further along the bar. You move a little to the left, Max." He was like a photographer arranging for a group picture.

"Talk to me, bright boy," Max said. "What do you think's going to happen?"

George did not say anything.

"I'll tell you," Max said. "We're going to kill a Swede. Do you know a big Swede named Ole Anderson?"

"Yes."

"He comes here to eat every night, don't he?"

"Sometimes he comes here."

"He comes here at six o'clock, don't he?"

"If he comes."

"We know all that, bright boy," Max said. "Talk about something else. Ever go to the movies?"

"Once in a while."

"You ought to go to the movies more. The movies are fine for a bright boy like you."

"What are you going to kill Ole Anderson for? What did he ever do to you?"

"He never had a chance to do anything to us. He never even seen us."

And he's only going to see us once," Al said from the kitchen.

"What are you going to kill him for, then?" George asked.

"We're killing him for a friend. Just to oblige a friend, bright boy."

"Shut up," said Al from the kitchen. "You talk too damn much."

"Well, I got to keep bright boy amused. Don't I, bright boy?"

"You talk too damn much," Al said. "The black and my bright boy are amused by themselves. I got them tied up like a couple of girl friends in the convent."

"I suppose you were in a convent."

"You never know."

"You were in a kosher convent. That's where you were."

George looked up at the clock.

"If anybody comes in you tell them the cook is off, and if they keep after it, you tell them you'll go back and cook yourself. Do you get that, bright boy?"

"All right," George said. "What you going to do with us afterward?"

"That'll depend," Max said. "That's one of those things you never know at the time."

George looked up at the dock. It was a quarter past six. The door from the street opened. A streetcar motorman came in.

"Hello, George," he said. "Can I get supper?"

"Sam's gone out," George said. "He'll be back in about half an hour."

"I'd better go up the street," the motorman said. George looked at the clock. It was twenty minutes past six.

"That was nice, bright boy," Max said. "You're a regular little gentleman."

"He knew I'd blow his head off," Al said from the kitchen.

"No," said Max. "It ain't that. Bright boy is nice. He's a nice boy. I like him."

At six-fifty-five George said: "He's not coming."

Two other people had been in the lunchroom. Once George had gone out to the kitchen and made a ham-and-egg sandwich "to go" that a man wanted to take with him. Inside the kitchen he saw Al, his derby hat tipped back, sitting on a stool beside the wicket with the muzzle of a sawed-off shotgun resting on the ledge. Nick and the cook were back to back in the corner, a towel tied in each of their mouths. George had cooked the sandwich, wrapped it up in oiled paper, put it in a bag, brought it in, and the man had paid for it and gone out.

"Bright boy can do everything," Max said. "He can cook and everything. You'd make some girl a nice wife, bright boy."

"Yes?" George said, "Your friend, Ole Anderson, isn't going to come."

"We'll give him ten minutes," Max said.

Max watched the mirror and the clock. The hands of the clock marked seven o'clock, and then five minutes past seven.

"Come on, Al," said Max. "We better go. He's not coming."

"Better give him five minutes," Al said from the kitchen.

In the five minutes a man came in, and George explained that the cook was sick.

"Why the hell don't you get another cook?" the man asked. "Aren't you running a lunch-counter?" He went out.

"Come on, Al," Max said.

"What about the two bright boys and the black?"

"They're all right."

"You think so?"

"Sure. We're through with it."

"I don't like it," said Al. "It's sloppy. You talk too much."

"Oh, what the hell," said Max. "We got to keep amused, haven't we?"

"You talk too much, all the same," Al said. He came out from the kitchen. The cut-off barrels of the shotgun made a slight bulge under the waist of his too tight-fitting overcoat. He straightened his coat with his gloved hands.

"So long, bright boy," he said to George. "You got a lot of luck."

"That's the truth," Max said. "You ought to play the races, bright boy."

The two of them went out the door. George watched them, through the window, pass under the arc-light and across the street. In their tight overcoats and derby hats they looked like a vaudeville team. George went back through the swinging door into the kitchen and untied Nick and the cook.

"I don't want any more of that," said Sam, the cook. "I don't want any more of that."

Nick stood up. He had never had a towel in his mouth before.

"Say," he said. "What the hell?" He was trying to swagger it off.

"They were going to kill Ole Anderson," George said. "They were going to shoot him when he came in to eat."

"Ole Anderson?"

"Sure."

The cook felt the corners of his mouth with his thumbs.

"They all gone?" he asked.

"Yeah," said George. "They're gone now."

"I don't like it," said the cook. "I don't like any of it at all."

"Listen," George said to Nick. "You better go see Ole Anderson."

"All right."

"You better not have anything to do with it at all," Sam, the cook, said. "You better stay way out of it."

"Don't go if you don't want to," George said.

"Mixing up in this ain't going to get you anywhere," the cook said. "You stay out of it."

"I'll go see him," Nick said to George. "Where does he live?"

The cook turned away.

"Little boys always know what they want to do," he said.

"He lives up at Hirsch's rooming-house," George said to Nick.

"I'll go up there."

Outside the arc-light shone through the bare branches of a tree. Nick walked up the street beside the car-tracks and turned at the next arc-light down a side-street. Three houses up the street was Hirsch's rooming-house. Nick walked up the two steps and pushed the bell. A woman came to the door.

"Is Ole Anderson here?"

"Do you want to see him?"

"Yes, if he's in."

Nick followed the woman up a flight of stairs and back to the end of a corridor. She knocked on the door.

"Who is it?"

"It's somebody to see you, Mr. Anderson," the woman said.

"It's Nick Adams."

"Come in."

Nick opened the door and went into the room. Ole Anderson was lying on the bed with all his clothes on. He had been a heavyweight prizefighter and he was too long for the bed. He lay with his head on two pillows. He did not look at Nick.

"What was it?" he asked.

"I was up at Henry's," Nick said, "and two fellows came in and tied up me and the cook, and they said they were going to kill you."

It sounded silly when he said it. Ole Anderson said nothing.

"They put us out in the kitchen," Nick went on. "They were going to shoot you when you came in to supper."

Ole Anderson looked at the wall and did not say anything.

"George thought I better come and tell you about it."

"There isn't anything I can do about it," Ole Anderson said.

"I'll tell you what they were like."

"I don't want to know what they were like," Ole Anderson

said. He looked at the wall. "Thanks for coming to tell me about it."

"That's all right."

Nick looked at the big man lying on the bed.

"Don't you want me to go and see the police?"

"No," Ole Anderson said. "That wouldn't do any good."

"Isn't there something I could do?"

"No. There ain't anything to do."

"Maybe it was just a bluff."

"No. It ain't just a bluff."

Ole Anderson rolled over toward the wall.

"The only thing is," he said, talking toward the wall, "I just can't make up my mind to go out. I been here all day."

"Couldn't you get out of town?"

"No," Ole Anderson said. "I'm through with all that running around."

He looked at the wall.

"There ain't anything to do now."

"Couldn't you fix it up some way?"

"No. I got in wrong." He talked in the same flat voice. "There ain't anything to do. After a while I'll make up my mind to go out."

"I better go back and see George," Nick said.

"So long," said Ole Anderson. He did not look toward Nick. "Thanks for coming around."

Nick went out. As he shut the door he saw Ole Anderson with all his clothes on, lying on the bed looking at the wall.

"He's been in his room all day," the landlady said downstairs. "I guess he don't feel well. I said to him: 'Mr. Anderson, you ought to go out and take a walk on a nice fall day like this,' but he didn't feel like it."

"He doesn't want to go out."

"I'm sorry he don't feel well," the woman said. "He's an awfully nice man. He was in the ring, you know."

"I know it."

"You'd never know it except from the way his face is," the woman said.

They stood talking just inside the street door. "He's just as gentle."

"Well, good night, Mrs. Hirsch,' Nick said.

"I'm not Mrs. Hirsch," the woman said. "She owns the place. I just look after it for her. I'm Mrs. Bell."

"Well, good night, Mrs. Bell," Nick said.

"Good night," the woman said.

Nick walked up the dark street to the corner under the arc-light, and then along the car-tracks to Henry's eating-house. George was inside, back of the counter.

"Did you see Ole?"

"Yes," said Nick. "He's in his room and he won't go out."

The cook opened the door from the kitchen when he heard Nick's voice.

"I don't even listen to it," he said and shut the door.

"Did you tell him about it?" George asked.

"Sure. I told him but he knows what it's all about."

"What's he going to do?"

"Nothing."

"They'll kill him."

"I guess they will."

"He must have got mixed up in something in Chicago."

"I guess so," said Nick.

"It's a hell of a thing!"

"It's an awful thing," Nick said.

They did not say anything. George reached down for a towel and wiped the counter.

"I wonder what he did?" Nick said.

"Double-crossed somebody. That's what they kill them for."

"I'm going to get out of this town," Nick said.

"Yes," said George. "That's a good thing to do."

"I can't stand to think about him waiting in the room and knowing he's going to get it. It's too damned awful."

"Well," said George, "you better not think about it."

An Occurrence at Owl Creek Bridge

Ambrose Bierce

A man stood upon a railroad bridge in northern Alabama, looking down into the swift water twenty feet below. The man's hands were behind his back, the wrists bound with a cord. A rope closely encircled his neck. It was attached to a stout cross-timber above his head and the slack fell to the level of his knees. Some loose boards laid upon the sleepers supporting the metals of the railway supplied a footing for him and his executioners—two private soldiers of the Federal army, directed by a sergeant who in civil life may have been a deputy sheriff. At a short remove upon the same temporary platform was an officer in the uniform of his rank, armed. He was a captain. A sentinel at each end of the bridge stood with his rifle in the position known as "support," that is to say, vertical in front of the left shoulder, the hammer resting on the forearm thrown straight across the chest—a formal and unnatural position, enforcing an erect carriage of the body. It did not appear to be the duty of these two men to know what was occurring at the center of the bridge; they merely blockaded the two ends of the foot planking that traversed it.

Beyond one of the sentinels nobody was in sight; the railroad ran straight away into a forest for a hundred yards, then, curving, was lost to view. Doubtless there was an outpost farther along. The other bank of the stream was open ground—a gentle acclivity topped with a stockade of vertical tree trunks, loopholed for rifles, with a single embrasure through which protruded the muzzle of a brass cannon commanding the bridge. Midway of the slope between the bridge and fort were the spectators—a single company of infantry in line, at "parade rest," the butts of the rifles on the ground, the barrels inclining slightly backward against the right shoulder, the hands crossed upon the stock. A lieutenant stood at the right of the line, the point of his sword upon the ground, his left hand resting upon his right. Excepting the group of four at the center of the bridge, not a man moved. The company faced the bridge, staring stonily, motionless. The sentinels, facing the banks of the stream, might have been statues to adorn the bridge. The captain stood with folded arms, silent, observing the work of his subordinates, but making no sign. Death is a dignitary who when he comes announced is to be received with formal manifestations of respect, even by those most familiar with him. In the code of military etiquette silence and fixity are forms of deference.

The man who was engaged in being hanged was apparently about thirty-five years of age. He was a civilian, if one might judge from his habit, which was that of a planter. His features were good—a straight nose, firm mouth, broad forehead, from which his long, dark hair was combed straight back, falling behind his ears to the collar of his well-fitting frock coat. He wore a mustache and pointed beard, but no whiskers; his eyes were large and dark gray, and had a kindly expression which one would hardly have expected in one whose neck was in the hemp. Evidently this was no vulgar assassin. The liberal military code makes provision for hanging many kinds of persons, and gentlemen are not excluded.

The preparations being complete, the two private soldiers stepped aside and each drew away the plank upon which he had been standing. The sergeant turned to the captain, saluted and placed himself immediately behind that officer, who in turn moved apart one pace. These movements left the condemned man and the sergeant standing on the two ends of the same plank, which spanned three of the cross-ties of the bridge. The end upon which the civilian stood almost, but not quite, reached a fourth. This plank had been held in place by the weight of the captain; it was now held by that of the sergeant. At a signal from the former the latter would step aside, the plank would tilt and the condemned man go down between two ties. The arrangement commended itself to his judgment as simple and effective. His face had not been covered nor his eyes bandaged. He looked a moment at his "unsteadfast footing," then let his gaze wander to the swirling water of the stream racing madly beneath his feet. A piece of dancing driftwood caught his attention and his eyes followed it down the current. How slowly it appeared to move, What a sluggish stream!

He closed his eyes in order to fix his last thoughts upon his wife and children. The water, touched to gold by the early sun, the brooding mists under the banks at some distance down the stream, the fort, the soldiers, the piece of drift—all had distracted him. And now he became conscious of a new disturbance. Striking through the thought of his dear ones was a sound which he could neither ignore nor understand, a sharp, distinct, metallic percussion like the stroke of a blacksmith's hammer upon the anvil; it had the same ringing quality. He wondered what it was, and whether immeasurably distant or near by—it seemed both. Its recurrence was regular, but as slow as the tolling of a death knell. He awaited each stroke with impatience and—he knew not why—apprehension. The intervals of silence grew progressively longer, the delays became maddening. With their greater infrequency the sounds increased in strength and sharpness. They hurt his ear like the thrust of a knife; he feared he would shriek. What he heard was the ticking of his watch.

He unclosed his eyes and saw again the water below him. "If I could free my hands," he thought, "I might throw off the noose and spring into the stream. By diving I could evade the bullets and, swimming vigorously, reach the bank, take to the woods and get away home. My home, thank God, is as yet outside their lines; my wife and little ones are still beyond the invader's farthest advance."

As these thoughts, which have here to be set down in words, were flashed into the doomed man's brain rather than evolved from it the captain nodded to the sergeant. The sergeant stepped aside.

II

Peyton Farquhar was a well-to-do planter, of an old and highly respected Alabama family. Being a slave owner and like other slave owners a politician he was naturally an original secessionist and ardently devoted to the Southern cause. Circumstances of an imperious nature, which it is unnecessary to relate here, had prevented him from taking service with the gallant army that had fought the disastrous campaigns ending with the fall of Corinth, and he chafed under the inglorious restraint, longing for the release of his energies, the larger life of the soldier, the opportunity for distinction. That opportunity, he felt, would come, as it comes to all in war time. Meanwhile he did what he could. No service was too humble for him to perform in aid of the South, no adventure too perilous for him to undertake if consistent with the character of a civilian who was at heart a soldier, and who in good faith and without too much qualification assented to at least a part of the frankly villainous dictum that all is fair in love and war.

One evening while Farquhar and his wife were sitting on a rustic bench near the entrance to his grounds, a gray-clad soldier rode up to the gate and asked for a drink of water. Mrs. Farquhar was only too happy to serve him with her own white hands. While she was fetching the water her husband approached the dusty horseman and inquired eagerly for news from the front.

"The Yanks are repairing the railroads," said the man, "and are getting ready for another advance. They have reached the Owl Creek bridge, put it in order and built a stockade on the north bank. The commandant has issued an order, which is posted everywhere, declaring that any civilian caught interfering with the railroad, its bridges, tunnels or trains will be summarily hanged. I saw the order."

"How far is it to the Owl Creek bridge?" Farquhar asked.

"About thirty miles."

"Is there no force on this side the creek?"

"Only a picket post half a mile out, on the railroad, and a single sentinel at this end of the bridge."

"Suppose a man—a civilian and student of hanging—should elude the picket post and perhaps get the better of the sentinel," said Farquhar, smiling, "what could he accomplish?"

The soldier reflected. "I was there a month ago," he replied. "I observed that the flood of last winter had lodged a great quantity of driftwood against the wooden pier at this end of the bridge. It is now dry and would burn like tow."

The lady had now brought the water, which the soldier drank. He thanked her ceremoniously, bowed to her husband and rode away. An hour later, after nightfall, he repassed the plantation, going northward in the direction from which he had come. He was a Federal scout.

III

As Peyton Farquhar fell straight downward through the bridge he lost consciousness and was as one already dead. From this state he was awakened—ages later, it seemed to him—by the pain of a sharp pressure upon his throat, followed by a sense of suffocation. Keen, poignant agonies seemed to shoot from his neck downward through every fiber of his body and limbs. These pains appeared to flash along well-defined lines of ramification and to beat with an inconceivably rapid periodicity. They seemed like streams of pulsating fire heating him to an intolerable temperature. As to his head, he was conscious of nothing but a feeling of fulness—of congestion. These sensations were unaccompanied by thought. The intellectual part of his nature was already effaced; he had power only to feel, and feeling was torment. He was conscious of motion. Encompassed in a luminous cloud, of which he was now merely the fiery heart, without material substance, he swung through unthinkable arcs of oscillation, like a vast pendulum. Then all at once, with terrible suddenness, the light about him shot upward with the noise of a loud splash; a frightful roaring was in his ears, and all was cold and dark. The power of thought was restored; he knew that the rope had broken and he had fallen into the stream. There was no additional strangulation; the noose about his neck was already suffocating him and kept the water from his lungs. To die of hanging at the bottom of a river!—the idea seemed to him ludicrous. He opened his eyes in the darkness and saw above him a gleam of light, but how distant, how inaccessible! He was still sinking, for the light became fainter and fainter until it was a mere glimmer. Then it began to grow and brighten, and he knew that he was rising toward the surface—knew it with reluctance, for he was now very comfortable. "To be hanged and drowned," he thought? "that is not so bad; but I do not wish to be shot. No; I will not be shot; that is not fair."

He was not conscious of an effort, but a sharp pain in his wrist apprised him that he was trying to free his hands. He gave the struggle his attention, as an idler might observe the feat of a juggler, without interest in the outcome. What splendid effort!—what magnificent, what superhuman strength! Ah, that was a fine endeavor! Bravo! The cord fell away; his arms parted and floated upward, the hands dimly seen on each side in the growing light. He watched them with a new interest as first one and then the other pounced upon the noose at his neck. They tore it away and thrust it fiercely aside, its undulations resembling those of a water snake. "Put it back, put it back!" He thought he shouted these words to his hands, for the undoing of the noose had been succeeded by the direst pang that he had yet experienced. His neck ached horribly; his brain was on fire; his heart, which had been fluttering faintly, gave a great leap, trying to force itself out at his mouth. His whole body was racked and wrenched with an insupportable anguish! But his disobedient hands gave no heed to the command. They beat the water vigorously with quick, downward strokes, forcing him to the surface. He felt his head emerge; his eyes were blinded by the sunlight; his chest expanded convulsively, and with a supreme and crowning agony his lungs engulfed a great draught of air, which instantly he expelled in a shriek!

He was now in full possession of his physical senses. They were, indeed, preternaturally keen and alert. Something in the awful disturbance of his organic system had so exalted and refined them that they made record of things never before perceived. He felt the ripples upon his face and heard their separate sounds as they struck. He looked at the forest on the bank of the stream, saw the individual trees, the leaves and the veining of each leaf—saw the very insects upon them: the locusts, the brilliant-bodied flies, the grey spiders stretching their webs from twig to twig. He noted the prismatic colors in all the dewdrops upon a million blades of grass. The humming of the gnats that danced above the eddies of the stream, the beating of the dragon flies' wings, the strokes of the water-spiders' legs, like oars which had lifted their boat—all these made audible music. A fish slid along beneath his eyes and he heard the rush of its body parting the water.

He had come to the surface facing down the stream; in a moment the visible world seemed to wheel slowly round, himself the pivotal point, and he saw the bridge, the fort, the soldiers upon the bridge, the captain, the sergeant, the two privates, his executioners. They were in silhouette against the blue sky. They shouted and gesticulated, pointing at him. The captain had drawn his pistol, but did not fire; the others were unarmed. Their movements were grotesque and horrible, their forms gigantic.

Suddenly he heard a sharp report and something struck the water smartly within a few inches of his head, spattering his face with spray. He heard a second report, and saw one of the sentinels with his rifle at his shoulder, a light cloud of blue smoke rising from the muzzle. The man in the water saw the eye of the man on the bridge gazing into his own through the sights of the rifle. He observed that it was a grey eye and remembered having read that grey eyes were keenest, and that all famous marksmen had them. Nevertheless, this one had missed.

A counter-swirl had caught Farquhar and turned him half round; he was again looking into the forest on the bank opposite the fort. The sound of a clear, high voice in a monotonous singsong now rang out behind him and came across the water with a distinctness that pierced and subdued all other sounds, even the beating of the ripples in his ears. Although no soldier, he had frequented camps enough to know the dread significance of that deliberate, drawling, aspirated chant; the lieutenant on shore was taking a part in the morning's work. How coldly and pitilessly—with what an even, calm intonation, presaging, and enforcing tranquillity in the men—with what accurately measured intervals fell those cruel words:

"Attention, company! . . . Shoulder arms! . . . Ready! . . . Aim! . . . Fire!"

Farquhar dived—dived as deeply as he could. The water roared in his ears like the voice of Niagara, yet he heard the dulled thunder of the volley and, rising again toward the surface, met shining bits of metal, singularly flattened, oscillating slowly downward. Some of them touched him on the face and hands, then fell away, continuing their descent. One lodged between his collar and neck; it was uncomfortably warm and he snatched it out.

As he rose to the surface, gasping for breath, he saw that he had been a long time under water; he was perceptibly farther down stream nearer to safety. The soldiers had almost finished reloading; the metal ramrods flashed all at once in the sunshine as they were drawn from the barrels, turned in the air, and thrust into their sockets. The two sentinels fired again, independently and ineffectually.

The hunted man saw all this over his shoulder; he was now swimming vigorously with the current. His brain was as energetic as his arms and legs; he thought with the rapidity of lightning.

"The officer," he reasoned, "will not make that martinet's error a second time. It is as easy to dodge a volley as a single shot. He has probably already given the command to fire at will. God help me, I cannot dodge them all!"

An appalling splash within two yards of him was followed by a loud, rushing sound, diminuendo, which seemed to travel back through the air to the fort and died in an explosion which stirred the very river to its deeps!

A rising sheet of water curved over him, fell down upon him, blinded him, strangled him! The cannon had taken a hand in the game. As he shook his head free from the commotion of the smitten water he heard the deflected shot humming through the air ahead, and in an instant it was cracking and smashing the branches in the forest beyond.

"They will not do that again," he thought; "the next time they will use a charge of grape. I must keep my eye upon the gun; the smoke will apprise me—the report arrives too late; it lags behind the missile. That is a good gun."

Suddenly he felt himself whirled round and round—spinning like a top. The water, the banks, the forests, the now distant bridge, fort and men—all were commingled and blurred. Objects were represented by their colors only; circular horizontal streaks of color—that was all he saw. He had been caught in a vortex and was being whirled on with a velocity of advance and gyration that made him giddy and sick. In a few moments he was flung upon the gravel at the foot of the left bank of the stream—the southern bank—and behind a projecting point which concealed him from his enemies. The sudden arrest of his motion, the abrasion of one of his hands on the gravel, restored him, and he wept with delight. He dug his fingers into the sand, threw it over himself in handfuls and audibly blessed it. It looked like diamonds, rubies, emeralds; he could think of nothing beautiful which it did not resemble. The trees upon the bank were giant garden plants; he noted a definite order in their arrangement, inhaled the fragrance of their blooms. A strange, roseate light shone through the spaces among their trunks and the wind made in their branches the music of Æolian harps. He had no wish to perfect his escape—was content to remain in that enchanting spot until retaken.

A whiz and rattle of grapeshot among the branches high above his head roused him from his dream. The baffled cannoneer had fired him a random farewell. He sprang to his feet, rushed up the sloping bank, and plunged into the forest.

All that day he traveled, laying his course by the rounding sun. The forest seemed interminable; nowhere did he discover a break in it, not even a woodman's road. He had not known that he lived in so wild a region. There was something uncanny in the revelation.

By nightfall he was fatigued, footsore, famishing. The thought of his wife and children urged him on. At last he found a road which led him in what he knew to be the right direction. It was as wide and straight as a city street, yet it seemed untraveled. No fields bordered it, no dwelling anywhere. Not so much as the barking of a dog suggested human habitation. The black bodies of the trees formed a straight wall on both sides, terminating on the horizon in a point, like a diagram in a lesson in perspective. Overhead, as he looked up through this rift in the wood, shone great garden stars looking unfamiliar and grouped in strange constellations. He was sure they were arranged in some order which had a secret and malign significance. The wood on either side was full of singular noises, among which—

once, twice, and again—he distinctly heard whispers in an unknown tongue.

His neck was in pain and lifting his hand to it found it horribly swollen. He knew that it had a circle of black where the rope had bruised it. His eyes felt congested; he could no longer close them. His tongue was swollen with thirst; he relieved its fever by thrusting it forward from between his teeth into the cold air. How softly the turf had carpeted the untraveled avenue—he could no longer feel the roadway beneath his feet!

Doubtless, despite his suffering, he had fallen asleep while walking, for now he sees another scene—perhaps he has merely recovered from a delirium. He stands at the gate of his own home. All is as he left it, and all bright and beautiful in the morning sunshine. He must have traveled the entire night. As he pushes open the gate and passes up the wide white walk, he sees a flutter of female garments; his wife, looking fresh and cool and sweet, steps down from the veranda to meet him. At the bottom of the steps she stands waiting, with a smile of ineffable joy, an attitude of matchless grace and dignity. Ah, how beautiful she is! He springs forward with extended arms. As he is about to clasp her he feels a stunning blow upon the back of the neck; a blinding white light blazes all about him with a sound like the shock of a cannon—then all is darkness and silence!

Peyton Farquhar was dead; his body, with a broken neck, swung gently from side to side beneath the timbers of the Owl Creek bridge.

The Country of the Blind

H. G. Wells

Three hundred miles and more from Chimborazo, one hundred from the snows of Cotopaxi, in the wildest wastes of Ecuador's Andes, there lies that mysterious mountain valley, cut off from the world of men, the Country of the Blind. Long years ago that valley lay so far open to the world that men might come at last through frightful gorges and over an icy pass into its equable meadows; and thither indeed men came, a family or so of Peruvian half-breeds fleeing from the lust and tyranny of an evil Spanish ruler. Then came the stupendous outbreak of Mindobamba, when it was night in Quito for seventeen days, and the water was boiling at Yaguachi and all the fish floating dying even as far as Guayaquil; everywhere along the Pacific slopes there were land-slips and swift thawings and sudden floods, and one whole side of the old Arauca crest slipped and came down in thunder, and cut off the Country of the Blind for ever from the exploring feet of men. But one of these early settlers had chanced to be on the hither side of the gorges when the world had so terribly shaken itself, and he perforce had to forget his wife and his child and all the friends and possessions he had left up there, and start life over again in the lower world. He started it again but ill, blindness overtook him, and he died of punishment in the mines; but the story he told begot a legend that lingers along the length of the Cordilleras of the Andes to this day.

He told of his reason for venturing back from that fastness, into which he had first been carried lashed to a llama, beside a vast bale of gear, when he was a child. The valley, he said, had in it all that the heart of man could desire—sweet water, pasture, and even climate, slopes of rich brown soil with tangles of a shrub that bore an excellent fruit, and on one side great hanging forests of pine that held the avalanches high. Far overhead, on three sides, vast cliffs of grey-green rock were capped by cliffs of ice; but the glacier stream came not to them but flowed away by the farther slopes, and only now and then huge ice masses fell on the valley side. In this valley it neither rained nor snowed, but the abundant springs gave a rich green pasture, that irrigation would spread over all the valley space. The settlers did well indeed there. Their beasts did well and multiplied, and but one thing marred their happiness. Yet it was enough to mar it greatly. A strange disease had come upon them, and had made all the children born to them there—and indeed, several older children also—blind. It was to seek some charm or antidote against this plague of blindness that he had with fatigue and danger and difficulty returned down the gorge. In those days, in such cases, men did not think of germs and infections but of sins; and it seemed to him that the reason of this affliction must lie in the negligence of these priestless immigrants to set up a shrine so soon as they entered the valley. He wanted a shrine—a handsome, cheap, effectual shrine—to be erected in the valley; he wanted relics and such-like potent things of faith, blessed objects and mysterious medals and prayers. In his wallet he had a bar of native silver for which he would not account; he insisted there was none in the valley with something of the insistence of an inexpert liar. They had all clubbed their money and ornaments together, having little need for such treasure up there, he said, to buy them holy help against their ill. I figure this dim-eyed young mountaineer, sunburnt, gaunt, and anxious, hat-brim clutched feverishly, a man all unused to the ways of the lower world, telling this story to some keen-eyed, attentive priest before the great convulsion; I can picture him presently seeking to return with pious and infallible remedies against that trouble, and the infinite dismay with which he must have faced the tumbled vastness where the gorge had once come out. But the rest of his story of mischances is lost to me, save that I know of his evil death after several years. Poor stray from that remoteness! The stream that had once made the gorge now bursts from the mouth of a rocky cave, and the legend his poor, ill-told story set going developed into the legend of a race of blind men somewhere "over there" one may still hear today.

And amidst the little population of that now isolated and forgotten valley the disease ran its course. The old became groping and purblind, the young saw but dimly, and the children that were born to them saw never at all. But life was very easy in that snow-rimmed basin, lost to all the world, with neither thorns nor briars, with no evil insects nor any beasts save the gentle breed of llamas they had lugged and thrust and followed up the beds of the shrunken rivers in the gorges up which they had come. The seeing had become purblind so gradually that they scarcely noted their loss. They guided the sightless youngsters hither and thither until they knew the whole Valley marvellously, and when at last sight died out among them the race lived on. They had even time to adapt themselves to the blind control of fire, which they made carefully in stoves of stone. They were a simple strain of people at the first, unlettered, only slightly touched with the Spanish civilisation, but with something of a tradition of the arts of old Peru and of its lost philosophy. Generation followed generation. They forgot many things; they devised many things. Their tradition of the greater world they came from became mythical in colour and uncertain. In all things save sight they were strong and able, and presently the chance of birth and heredity sent one who had an original mind and who could talk and persuade among them, and then afterwards another. These two passed, leaving their effects, and the little community grew in numbers and in understanding, and met and settled social and economic problems that arose. Generation followed generation. Generation followed generation. There came a time when a child was born who was fifteen generations from that ancestor who went out of the valley with a bar of silver to seek God's aid, and who never returned. Thereabouts it chanced that a man came into this community from the outer world. And this is the story of that man.

He was a mountaineer from the country near Quito, a man who had been down to the sea and had seen the world, a reader of books in an original way, an acute and enterprising man, and he was taken on by a party of Englishmen who had come out to Ecuador to climb mountains, to replace one of their three Swiss guides who had fallen ill. He climbed here and he climbed there, and then came the attempt on Parascotopetl, the Matterhorn of the Andes, in which he was lost to the outer world. The story of the accident has been written a dozen times. Pointer's narrative is the best. He tells how the little party worked their difficult and almost vertical way up to the very foot of the last and greatest precipice, and how they built a night shelter amidst the snow upon a little shelf of rock, and, with a touch of real dramatic power, how presently they found Nunez had gone from them. They shouted, and there was no reply; shouted and whistled, and for the rest of that night they slept no more.

As the morning broke they saw the traces of his fall. It seems impossible he could have uttered a sound. He had slipped eastward towards the unknown side of the mountain; far below he had struck a steep slope of snow, and ploughed his way down it in the midst of a snow avalanche. His track went straight to the edge of a frightful precipice, and beyond that everything was hidden. Far, far below, and hazy with distance, they could see trees rising out of a narrow, shut-in valley—the lost Country of the Blind. But they did not know it was the lost Country of the Blind, nor distinguish it in any way from any other narrow streak of upland valley. Unnerved by this disaster, they abandoned their attempt in the afternoon, and Pointer was called away to the war before he could make another attack. To this day Parascotopetl lifts an unconquered crest, and Pointer's shelter crumbles unvisited amidst the snows.

And the man who fell survived.

At the end of the slope he fell a thousand feet, and came down in the midst of a cloud of snow upon a snow slope even steeper than the one above. Down this he was whirled, stunned and insensible, but without a bone broken in his body; and then at last came to gentler slopes, and at last rolled out and lay still, buried amidst a softening heap of the white masses that had accompanied and saved him. He came to himself with a dim fancy that he was ill in bed; then realised his position with a mountaineer's intelligence, and worked himself loose and, after a rest or so, out until he saw the stars. He rested flat upon his chest for a space, wondering where he was and what had happened to him. He explored his limbs, and discovered that several of his buttons were gone and his coat turned over his head. His knife had gone from his pocket and his hat was lost, though he had tied it under his chin. He recalled that he had been looking for loose stones to raise his piece of the shelter wall. His ice-axe had disappeared.

He decided he must have fallen, and looked up to see, exaggerated by the ghastly light of the rising moon, the tremendous flight he had taken. For a while he lay, gazing blankly at that vast pale cliff towering above, rising moment by moment out of a subsiding tide of darkness. Its phantasmal, mysterious beauty held him for a space, and then he was seized with a paroxysm of sobbing laughter . . .

After a great interval of time he became aware that he was near the lower edge of the snow. Below, down what was now a moonlit and practicable slope, he saw the dark and broken appearance of rock-strewn turf. He struggled to his feet, aching in every joint and limb, got down painfully from the heaped loose snow about him, went downward until he was on the turf, and there dropped rather than lay beside a boulder, drank deep from the flask in his inner pocket, and instantly fell asleep . . .

He was awakened by the singing of birds in the trees far below.

He sat up and perceived he was on a little alp at the foot of a vast precipice, that was grooved by the gully down which he and his snow had come. Over against him another wall of rock reared itself against the sky. The gorge between these precipices ran east and west and was full of the morning sunlight, which lit to the westward the mass of fallen mountain that closed the descending gorge. Below him it seemed there was a precipice equally steep, but behind the snow in the gully he found a sort of chimney-cleft dripping with snow-water down which a desperate man might venture. He found it easier than it seemed, and came at last to another desolate alp, and then after a rock climb of no particular difficulty to a steep slope of trees. He took his bearings and turned his face up the gorge, for he saw it opened out above upon green meadows, among which he now glimpsed quite distinctly a cluster of stone huts of unfamiliar fashion. At times his progress was like clambering along the face of a wall, and after a time the rising sun ceased to strike along the gorge, the voices of the singing birds died away, and the air grew cold and dark about him. But the distant valley with its houses was all the brighter for that. He came presently to talus, and among the rocks he noted—for he was an observant man—an unfamiliar fern that seemed to clutch out of the crevices with intense green hands. He picked a frond or so and gnawed its stalk and found it helpful.

About midday he came at last out of the throat of the gorge into the plain and the sunlight. He was stiff and weary; he sat down in the shadow of a rock, filled up his flask with water from a spring and drank it down, and remained for a time resting before he went on to the houses.

They were very strange to his eyes, and indeed the whole aspect of that valley became, as he regarded it, queerer and more unfamiliar. The greater part of its surface was lush green meadow, starred with many beautiful flowers, irrigated with extraordinary care, and bearing evidence of systematic cropping piece by piece. High up and ringing the valley about was a wall, and what appeared to be a circumferential water-channel, from which the little trickles of water that fed the meadow plants came, and on the higher slopes above this flocks of llamas cropped the scanty herbage. Sheds, apparently shelters or feeding-places for the llamas, stood against the boundary wall here and there. The irrigation streams ran together into a main channel down the centre of the valley, and this was enclosed on either side by a wall breast high. This gave a singularly urban quality to this secluded place, a quality that was greatly enhanced by the fact that a number of paths paved with black and white stones, and each with a curious little kerb at the side, ran hither and thither in an orderly manner. The houses of the central village were quite unlike the casual and higgledy-piggledy agglomeration of the mountain villages he knew; they stood in a continuous row on either side of a central street of astonishing cleanness; here and there their particoloured facade was pierced by a door, and not a solitary window broke their even frontage. They were particoloured with extraordinary irregularity, smeared with a sort of plaster that was sometimes grey, sometimes drab, sometimes slate-coloured or dark brown; and it was the sight of this wild plastering first brought the word "blind" into the thoughts of the explorer. "The good man who did that," he thought, "must have been as blind as a bat."

He descended a steep place, and so came to the wall and channel that ran about the valley, near where the latter spouted out its surplus contents into the deeps of the gorge in a thin and wavering thread of cascade. He could now see a number of men and women resting on piled heaps of grass, as if taking a siesta, in the remoter part of the meadow, and nearer the village a number of recumbent children, and then nearer at hand three men carrying pails on yokes along a little path that ran from the encircling wall towards the houses. These latter were clad in garments of llama cloth and boots and belts of leather, and they wore caps of cloth with back and ear flaps. They followed one another in single file, walking slowly and yawning as they walked, like men who have been up all night. There was something so reassuringly prosperous and respectable in their bearing that after a moment's hesitation Nunez stood forward as conspicuously as possible upon his rock, and gave vent to a mighty shout that echoed round the valley.

The three men stopped, and moved their heads as though they were looking about them. They turned their faces this way and that, and Nunez gesticulated with freedom. But they did not appear to see him for all his gestures, and after a time, directing themselves towards the mountains far away to the right, they shouted as if in answer. Nunez bawled again, and then once more, and as he gestured ineffectually the word "blind" came up to the top of his thoughts. "The fools must be blind," he said.

When at last, after much shouting and wrath, Nunez crossed the stream by a little bridge, came through a gate in the wall, and approached them, he was sure that they were blind. He was sure that this was the Country of the Blind of which the legends told. Conviction had sprung upon him, and a sense of great and rather enviable adventure. The three stood side by side, not looking at him, but with their ears directed towards him, judging him by his unfamiliar steps. They stood close together like men a little afraid, and he could see their eyelids closed and sunken, as though the very balls beneath had shrunk away. There was an expression near awe on their faces.

"A man," one said, in hardly recognisable Spanish—"a man it is—a man or a spirit—coming down from the rocks."

But Nunez advanced with the confident steps of a youth who enters upon life. All the old stories of the lost valley and the

Country of the Blind had come back to his mind, and through his thoughts ran this old proverb, as if it were a refrain—

"In the Country of the Blind the One-eyed Man is King."

"In the Country of the Blind the One-eyed Man is King."

And very civilly he gave them greeting. He talked to them and used his eyes.

"Where does he come from, brother Pedro?" asked one.

"Down out of the rocks."

"Over the mountains I come," said Nunez, "out of the country beyond there—where men can see. From near Bogota, where there are a hundred thousands of people, and where the city passes out of sight."

"Sight?" muttered Pedro. "Sight?"

"He comes," said the second blind man, "out of the rocks."

The cloth of their coats Nunez saw was curiously fashioned, each with a different sort of stitching.

They startled him by a simultaneous movement towards him, each with a hand outstretched. He stepped back from the advance of these spread fingers.

"Come hither," said the third blind man, following his motion and clutching him neatly.

And they held Nunez and felt him over, saying no word further until they had done so.

"Carefully," he cried, with a finger in his eye, and found they thought that organ, with its fluttering lids, a queer thing in him. They went over it again.

"A strange creature, Correa," said the one called Pedro. "Feel the coarseness of his hair. Like a llama's hair."

"Rough he is as the rocks that begot him," said Correa, investigating Nunez's unshaven chin with a soft and slightly moist hand. "Perhaps he will grow finer." Nunez struggled a little under their examination, but they gripped him firm.

"Carefully," he said again.

"He speaks," said the third man. "Certainly he is a man."

"Ugh!" said Pedro, at the roughness of his coat.

"And you have come into the world?" asked Pedro.

"*Out* of the world. Over mountains and glaciers; right over above there, half-way to the sun. Out of the great big world that goes down, twelve days' journey to the sea."

They scarcely seemed to heed him. "Our fathers have told us men may be made by the forces of Nature," said Correa. "It is the warmth of things and moisture, and rottenness—rottenness."

"Let us lead him to the elders," said Pedro.

"Shout first," said Correa, "lest the children be afraid . . . This is a marvellous occasion."

So they shouted, and Pedro went first and took Nunez by the hand to lead him to the houses.

He drew his hand away. "I can see," he said.

"See?" said Correa.

"Yes, see," said Nunez, turning towards him, and stumbled against Pedro's pail.

"His senses are still imperfect," said the third blind man. "He stumbles, and talks unmeaning words. Lead him by the hand."

"As you will," said Nunez, and was led along, laughing.

It seemed they knew nothing of sight.

Well, all in good time he would teach them.

He heard people shouting, and saw a number of figures gathering together in the middle roadway of the village.

He found it tax his nerve and patience more than he had anticipated, that first encounter with the population of the Country of the Blind. The place seemed larger as he drew near to it, and the smeared plasterings queerer, and a crowd of children and men and women (the women and girls, he was pleased to note, had some of them quite sweet faces, for all that their eyes were shut and sunken) came about him, holding on to him, touching him with soft, sensitive hands, smelling at him, and listening at every word he spoke. Some of the maidens and children, however, kept aloof as if afraid, and indeed his voice seemed coarse and rude beside their softer notes. They mobbed him. His three guides kept close to him with an effect of proprietorship, and said again and again, "A wild man out of the rock."

"Bogota," he said. "Bogota. Over the mountain crests."

"A wild man—using wild words," said Pedro. "Did you hear that—*Bogota?* His mind is hardly formed yet. He has only the beginnings of speech."

A little boy nipped his hand. "Bogota!" he said mockingly.

"Ay! A city to your village. I come from the great world—where men have eyes and see."

"His name's Bogota," they said.

"He stumbled," said Correa, "stumbled twice as we came hither."

"Bring him to the elders."

And they thrust him suddenly through a doorway into a room as black as pitch, save at the end there faintly glowed a fire. The crowd closed in behind him and shut out all but the faintest glimmer of day, and before he could arrest himself he had fallen headlong over the feet of a seated man. His arm, outflung, struck the face of someone else as he went down; he felt the soft impact of features and heard a cry of anger, and for a moment he struggled against a number of hands that clutched him. It was a one-sided fight. An inkling of the situation came to him, and he lay quiet.

"I fell down," he said; "I couldn't see in this pitchy darkness."

There was a pause as if the unseen persons about him tried to understand his words. Then the voice of Correa said: "He is but newly formed. He stumbles as he walks and mingles words that mean nothing with his speech."

Others also said things about him that he heard or understood imperfectly.

"May I sit up?" he asked, in a pause. "I will not struggle against you again."

They consulted and let him rise.

The voice of an older man began to question him, and Nunez found himself trying to explain the great world out of which he had fallen, and the sky and mountains and sight and such-like marvels, to these elders who sat in darkness in the Country of the Blind. And they would believe and understand nothing whatever he told them, a thing quite outside his expectation. They would not even understand many of his words. For fourteen generations these people had been blind and cut off from all the seeing world; the names for all the things of sight had faded and changed; the story of the outer world was faded and changed to a child's story; and they had ceased to concern themselves with anything beyond the rocky slopes above their circling wall. Blind men of genius had arisen among them and questioned the shreds of belief and tradition they had brought with them from their seeing days, and had dismissed all these things as idle fancies, and replaced them with new and saner explanations. Much of their imagination had shrivelled with their eyes, and they had made for themselves new imaginations with their ever more sensitive ears and finger-tips. Slowly Nunez realised this; that his expectation of wonder and reverence at his origin and his gifts was not to be borne out; and after his poor attempt to explain sight to them had been set aside as the confused version of a new-made being describing the marvels of his incoherent sensations, he subsided, a little dashed, into listening to their instruction. And the eldest of the blind men explained to him life and philosophy and religion, how that the world (meaning their valley) had been first an empty hollow in the rocks, and then had come, first, inanimate things without the gift of touch, and llamas and a few other creatures that had little sense, and then men, and at last angels, whom one could hear singing and making fluttering sounds, but whom no one could touch at all, which puzzled Nunez greatly until he thought of the birds.

He went on to tell Nunez how this time had been divided into the warm and the cold, which are the blind equivalents of day and night, and how it was good to sleep in the warm and work during the cold, so that now, but for his advent, the whole town of the blind would have been asleep. He said Nunez must have been specially created to learn and serve the wisdom, they had acquired, and that for all his mental incoherency and stumbling behaviour he must have courage, and do his best to learn, and at that all the people in the doorway murmured encouragingly. He said the night—for the blind call their day night—was now far gone, and it behoved every one to go back to sleep. He asked Nunez if he knew how to sleep, and Nunez said he did, but that before sleep he wanted food.

They brought him food—llama's milk in a bowl, and rough salted bread—and led him into a lonely place, to eat out of their hearing, and afterwards to slumber until the chill of the mountain evening roused them to begin their day again. But Nunez slumbered not at all.

Instead, he sat up in the place where they had left him, resting his limbs and turning the unanticipated circumstances of his arrival over and over in his mind.

Every now and then he laughed, sometimes with amusement, and sometimes with indignation.

"Unformed mind!" he said. "Got no senses yet! They little know they've been insulting their heaven-sent king and master. I see I must bring them to reason. Let me think—let me think."

He was still thinking when the sun set.

Nunez had an eye for all beautiful things, and it seemed to him that the glow upon the snowfields and glaciers that rose about the valley on every side was the most beautiful thing he had ever seen. His eyes went from that inaccessible glory to the village and irrigated fields, fast sinking into the twilight, and suddenly a wave of emotion took him, and he thanked God from the bottom of his heart that the power of sight had been given him.

He heard a voice calling to him from out of the village. "Ya ho there, Bogota! Come hither!"

At that he stood up smiling. He would show these people once and for all what sight would do for a man. They would seek him, but not find him.

"You move not, Bogota," said the voice.

He laughed noiselessly, and made two stealthy steps aside from the path.

"Trample not on the grass, Bogota; that is not allowed."

Nunez had scarcely heard the sound he made himself. He stopped amazed.

The owner of the voice came running up the piebald path towards him.

He stepped back into the pathway. "Here I am," he said.

"Why did you not come when I called you?" said the blind man. "Must you be led like a child? Cannot you hear the path as you walk?"

Nunez laughed. "I can see it," he said.

"There is no such word as *see,*" said the blind man, after a pause. "Cease this folly, and follow the sound of my feet."

Nunez followed, a little annoyed.

"My time will come," he said.

"You'll learn," the blind man answered. "There is much to learn in the world."

"Has no one told you, 'In the Country of the Blind the One-eyed Man is King'?"

"What is blind?" asked the blind man carelessly over his shoulder.

Four days passed, and the fifth found the King of the Blind still incognito, as a clumsy and useless stranger among his subjects.

It was, he found, much more difficult to proclaim himself than he had supposed, and in the meantime, while he meditated his *coup d'état,* he did what he was told and learnt the manners and customs of the Country of the Blind. He found working and going about at night a particularly irksome thing, and he decided that that should be the first thing he would change.

They led a simple, laborious life, these people, with all the elements of virtue and happiness, as these things can be understood by men. They toiled, but not oppressively; they had food and clothing sufficient for their needs; they had days and seasons of rest; they made much of music and singing, and there was love among them, and little children.

It was marvellous with what confidence and precision they went about their ordered world. Everything, you see, had been made to fit their needs; each of the radiating paths of the valley area had a constant angle to the others, and was distinguished by a special notch upon its kerbing; all obstacles and irregularities of path or meadow had long since been cleared away; all their methods and procedure arose naturally from their special needs. Their senses had become marvellously acute; they could hear and judge the slightest gesture of a man a dozen paces away—could hear the very beating of his heart. Intonation had long replaced expression with them, and touches gesture, and their work with hoe and spade and fork was as free and confident as garden work can be. Their sense of smell was extraordinarily fine; they could distinguish individual differences as readily as a dog can, and they went about the tending of the llamas, who lived among the rocks above and came to the wall for food and shelter, with ease and confidence. It was only when at last Nunez sought to assert himself that he found how easy and confident their movements could be.

He rebelled only after he had tried persuasion.

He tried at first on several occasions to tell them of sight. "Look you here, you people," he said. "There are things you do not understand in me."

Once or twice one or two of them attended to him; they sat with faces downcast and ears turned intelligently towards him, and he did his best to tell them what it was to see. Among his hearers was a girl, with eyelids less red and sunken than the others, so that one could almost fancy she was hiding eyes, whom especially he hoped to persuade. He spoke of the beauties of sight, of watching the mountains, of the sky and the sunrise, and they heard him with amused incredulity that presently became condemnatory. They told him there were indeed no mountains at all, but that the end of the rocks where the llamas grazed was indeed the end of the world; thence sprang a cavernous roof of the universe, from which the dew and the avalanches fell; and when he maintained stoutly the world had neither end nor roof such as they supposed, they said his thoughts were wicked. So far as he could describe sky and clouds and stars to them it seemed to them a hideous void, a terrible blankness in the place of the smooth roof to things in which they believed—it was an article of faith with them that the cavern roof was exquisitely smooth to the touch. He saw that in some manner he shocked them, and gave up that aspect of the matter altogether, and tried to show them the practical value of sight. One morning he saw Pedro in the path called Seventeen and coming towards the central houses, but still too far off for hearing or scent, and he told them as much. "In a little while," he prophesied, "Pedro will be here." An old man remarked that Pedro had no business on path Seventeen, and then, as if in confirmation, that individual as he drew near turned and went transversely into path Ten, and so back with nimble paces towards the outer wall. They mocked Nunez when Pedro did not arrive, and afterwards, when he asked Pedro questions to clear his character, Pedro denied and outfaced him, and was afterwards hostile to him.

Then he induced them to let him go a long way up the sloping meadows towards the wall with one complacent individual, and to him he promised to describe all that happened among the houses. He noted certain goings and comings, but the things that really seemed to signify to these people happened inside of or behind the windowless houses—the only things they took note of to test him by—and of these he could see or tell nothing; and it was after the failure of this attempt, and the ridicule they could not repress, that he resorted to force. He thought of seizing a spade and suddenly smiting one or two of them to earth, and so in fair combat showing the advantage of eyes. He went so far with that resolution as to seize his spade, and then he discovered a new thing about himself, and that was that it was impossible for him to hit a blind man in cold blood.

He hesitated, and found them all aware that he had snatched up the spade. They stood alert, with their heads on one side, and bent ears towards him for what he would do next.

"Put that spade down," said one, and he felt a sort of helpless horror. He came near obedience.

Then he thrust one backwards against a house wall, and fled past him and out of the village.

He went athwart one of their meadows, leaving a track of trampled grass behind his feet, and presently sat down by the side of one of their ways. He felt something of the buoyancy that comes to all men in the beginning of a fight, but more perplexity. He began to realise that you cannot even fight happily with creatures who stand upon a different mental basis to yourself. Far away he saw a number of men carrying spades and sticks come out of the street of houses, and advance in a spreading line along the several paths towards him. They advanced slowly, speaking frequently to one another, and ever and again the whole cordon would halt and sniff the air and listen.

The first time they did this Nunez laughed. But afterwards he did not laugh.

One struck his trail in the meadow grass, and came stooping and feeling his way along it.

For five minutes he watched the slow extension of the cordon, and then his vague disposition to do something forthwith became frantic. He stood up, went a pace or so towards the circumferential wall, turned, and went back a little way. There they all stood in a crescent, still and listening.

He also stood still, gripping his spade very tightly in both hands. Should he charge them?

The pulse in his ears ran into the rhythm of "In the Country of the Blind the One-eyed Man is King!"

Should he charge them?

He looked back at the high and unclimbable wall behind—

unclimbable because of its smooth plastering, but withal pierced with many little doors, and at the approaching line of seekers. Behind these others were now coming out of the street of houses.

Should he charge them?

"Bogota!" called one. "Bogota! where are you?"

He gripped his spade still tighter, and advanced down the meadows towards the place of habitations, and directly he moved they converged upon him. "I'll hit them if they touch me," he swore; "by Heaven, I will. I'll hit." He called aloud, "Look here, I'm going to do what I like in this valley. Do you hear? I'm going to do what I like and go where I like!"

They were moving in upon him quickly, groping, yet moving rapidly. It was like playing blind man's buff, with everyone blindfolded except one. "Get hold of him!" cried one. He found himself in the arc of a loose curve of pursuers. He felt suddenly he must be active and resolute.

"You don't understand," he cried in a voice that was meant to be great and resolute, and which broke. "You are blind, and I can see. Leave me alone!"

"Bogota! Put down that spade, and come off the grass!"

The last order, grotesque in its urban familiarity, produced a gust of anger.

"I'll hurt you," he said, sobbing with emotion. "By Heaven, I'll hurt you. Leave me alone!"

He began to run, not knowing clearly where to run. He ran from the nearest blind man, because it was a horror to hit him. He stopped, and then made a dash to escape from their closing ranks. He made for where a gap was wide, and the men on either side, with a quick perception of the approach of his paces, rushed in on one another. He sprang forward, and then saw he must be caught, and *swish!* the spade had struck. He felt the soft thud of hand and arm, and the man was down with a yell of pain, and he was through.

Through! And then he was close to the street of houses again, and blind men, whirling spades and stakes, were running with a sort of reasoned swiftness hither and thither.

He heard steps behind him just in time, and found a tall man rushing forward and swiping at the sound of him. He lost his nerve, hurled his spade a yard wide at his antagonist, and whirled about and fled, fairly yelling as he dodged another.

He was panic-stricken. He ran furiously to and fro, dodging when there was no need to dodge, and in his anxiety to see on every side of him at once, stumbling. For a moment he was down and they heard his fall. Far away in the circumferential wall a little doorway looked like heaven, and he set off in a wild rush for it. He did not even look round at his pursuers until it was gained, and he had stumbled across the bridge, clambered a little way among the rocks, to the surprise and dismay of a young llama, who went leaping out of sight, and lay down sobbing for breath.

And so his *coup d'état* came to an end.

He stayed outside the wall of the valley of the Blind for two nights and days without food or shelter, and meditated upon the unexpected. During these meditations he repeated very frequently and always with a profounder note of derision the exploded proverb: "In the Country of the Blind the One-Eyed Man is King." He thought chiefly of ways of fighting and conquering these people, and it grew clear that for him no practicable way was possible. He had no weapons, and now it would be hard to get one.

The canker of civilisation had got to him even in Bogota, and he could not find it in himself to go down and assassinate a blind man. Of course, if he did that, he might then dictate terms on the threat of assassinating them all. But—sooner or later he must sleep! . . .

He tried also to find food among the pine trees, to be comfortable under pine boughs while the frost fell at night, and—with less confidence—to catch a llama by artifice in order to try to kill it—perhaps by hammering it with a stone—and so finally, perhaps, to eat some of it. But the llamas had a doubt of him and regarded him with distrustful brown eyes, and spat when he drew near. Fear came on him the second day and fits of shivering. Finally he crawled down to the wall of the Country of the Blind and tried to make terms. He crawled along by the stream, shouting, until two blind men came out to the gate and talked to him.

"I was mad," he said. "But I was only newly made."

They said that was better.

He told them he was wiser now, and repented of all he had done.

Then he wept without intention, for he was very weak and ill now, and they took that as a favourable sign.

They asked him if he still thought he could "*see.*"

"No," he said. "That was folly. The word means nothing—less than nothing!"

They asked him what was overhead.

"About ten times ten the height of a man there is a roof above the world—of rock—and very, very smooth." . . . He burst again into hysterical tears. "Before you ask me any more, give me some food or I shall die."

He expected dire punishments, but these blind people were capable of toleration. They regarded his rebellion as but one more proof of his general idiocy and inferiority; and after they had whipped him they appointed him to do the simplest and heaviest work they had for anyone to do, and he, seeing no other way of living, did submissively what he was told.

He was ill for some days, and they nursed him kindly. That refined his submission. But they insisted on his lying in the dark, and that was a great misery. And blind philosophers came and talked to him of the wicked levity of his mind, and reproved him so impressively for his doubts about the lid of rock that covered their cosmic casserole that he almost doubted whether indeed he was not the victim of hallucination in not seeing it overhead.

So Nunez became a citizen of the Country of the Blind, and these people ceased to be a generalised people and became individualities and familiar to him, while the world beyond the mountains became more and more remote and unreal. There was Yacob, his master, a kindly man when not annoyed; there was Pedro, Yacob's nephew; and there was Medina-saroté, who was the youngest daughter of Yacob. She was little esteemed in the world of the blind, because she had a clear-cut face, and lacked that satisfying, glossy smoothness that is the blind man's ideal of feminine beauty; but Nunez thought her beautiful at first, and presently the most beautiful thing in the whole creation. Her closed eyelids were not sunken and red after the common way of the valley, but lay as though they might open again at any moment; and she had long eyelashes, which were considered a grave disfigurement. And her voice was strong, and did not satisfy the acute hearing of the valley swains. So that she had no lover.

There came a time when Nunez thought that, could he win her, he would be resigned to live in the valley for all the rest of his days.

He watched her; he sought opportunities of doing her little services, and presently he found that she observed him. Once at a rest-day gathering they sat side by side in the dim starlight, and the music was sweet. His hand came upon hers and he dared to clasp it. Then very tenderly she returned his pressure. And one day, as they were at their meal in the darkness, he felt her hand very softly seeking him, and as it chanced the fire leapt then and he saw the tenderness of her face.

He sought to speak to her.

He went to her one day when she was sitting in the summer moonlight spinning. The light made her a thing of silver and mystery. He sat down at her feet and told her he loved her, and told her how beautiful she seemed to him. He had a lover's voice, he spoke with a tender reverence that came near to awe, and she had never before been touched by adoration. She made him no definite answer, but it was clear his words pleased her.

After that he talked to her whenever he could take an opportunity. The valley became the world for him, and the world beyond the mountains where men lived in sunlight seemed no more than a fairy tale he would some day pour into her ears. Very tentatively and timidly he spoke to her of sight.

Sight seemed to her the most poetical of fancies, and she listened to his description of the stars and the mountains and her own sweet white-lit beauty as though it was a guilty indulgence. She did not believe, she could only half understand, but she was mysteriously delighted, and it seemed to him that she completely understood.

His love lost its awe and took courage. Presently he was for demanding her of Yacob and the elders in marriage, but she became fearful and delayed. And it was one of her elder sisters who first told Yacob that Medina-saroté and Nunez were in love.

There was from the first very great opposition to the marriage of Nunez and Medina-saroté; not so much because they valued her as because they held him as a being apart, an idiot, incompetent thing below the permissible level of a man. Her sisters opposed it bitterly as bringing discredit on them all; and old Yacob, though he had formed a sort of liking for his clumsy, obedient serf, shook his head and said the thing could not be. The young men were all angry at the idea of corrupting the race, and one went so far as to revile and strike Nunez. He struck back. Then for the first time he found an advantage in seeing, even by twilight, and after that fight was over no one was disposed to raise a hand against him. But they still found his marriage impossible.

Old Yacob had a tenderness for his last little daughter, and was grieved to have her weep upon his shoulder.

"You see, my dear, he's an idiot. He has delusions; he can't do anything right."

"I know," wept Medina-saroté. "But he's better than he was. He's getting better. And he's strong, dear father, and kind—stronger and kinder than any I other man in the world. And he loves me—and, father, I love him."

Old Yacob was greatly distressed to find her inconsolable, and, besides—what made it more distressing—he liked Nunez for many things. So he went and sat in the windowless council-chamber with the other elders and watched the trend of the talk, and said, at the proper time, "He's better than he was. Very likely, some day, we shall find him as sane as ourselves."

Then afterwards one of the elders, who thought deeply, had an idea. He was the great doctor among these people, their medicine-man, and he had a very philosophical and inventive mind, and the idea of curing Nunez of his peculiarities appealed to him. One day when Yacob was present he returned to the topic of Nunez.

"I have examined Bogota," he said, "and the case is clearer to me. I think very probably he might be cured."

"That is what I have always hoped," said old Yacob.

"His brain is affected," said the blind doctor.

The elders murmured assent.

"Now, *what* affects it?"

"Ah!" said old Yacob.

"*This,*" said the doctor, answering his own question. "Those queer things that are called the eyes, and which exist to make an agreeable soft depression in the face, are diseased, in the case of Bogota, in such a way as to affect his brain. They are greatly distended, he has eyelashes, and his eyelids move, and consequently his brain is in a state of constant irritation and distraction."

"Yes?" said old Yacob. "Yes?"

"And I think I may say with reasonable certainty that, in order to cure him completely, all that we need do is a simple and easy surgical operation—namely, to remove these irritant bodies."

"And then he will be sane?"

"Then he will be perfectly sane, and a quite admirable citizen."

"Thank Heaven for science!" said old Yacob, and went forth at once to tell Nunez of his happy hopes.

But Nunez's manner of receiving the good news struck him as being cold and disappointing.

"One might think," he said, "from the tone you take, that you did not care for my daughter."

It was Medina-saroté who persuaded Nunez to face the blind surgeons.

"*You* do not want me," he said, "to lose my gift of sight?"

She shook her head.

"My world is sight."

Her head drooped lower.

"There are the beautiful things, the beautiful little things—the flowers, the lichens among the rocks, the lightness and softness on a piece of fur, the far sky with its drifting down of clouds, the sunsets and the stars. And there is *you*. For you alone it is good to have sight, to see your sweet, serene face, your kindly lips, your dear, beautiful hands folded together . . . It is these eyes of mine you won, these eyes that hold me to you, that these idiots seek. Instead, I must touch you, hear you, and never see you again. I must come under that roof of rock and stone and darkness, that horrible roof under which your imagination stoops . . . No; you would not have me do that?"

A disagreeable doubt had arisen in him. He stopped, and left the thing a question.

"I wish," she said, "sometimes—" She paused.

"Yes," said he, a little apprehensively.

"I wish sometimes—you would not talk like that."

"Like what?"

"I know it's pretty—it's your imagination. I love it, but *now*—"

He felt cold. "*Now?*" he said faintly.

She sat quite still.

"You mean—you think—I should be better, better perhaps—"

He was realising things very swiftly. He felt anger, indeed, anger at the dull course of fate, but also sympathy for her lack of understanding—a sympathy near akin to pity.

"*Dear,*" he said, and he could see by her whiteness how intensely her spirit pressed against the things she could not say. He put his arms about her, he kissed her ear, and they sat for a time in silence.

"If I were to consent to this?" he said at last, in a voice that was very gentle.

She flung her arms about him, weeping wildly. "Oh, if you would," she sobbed, "if only you would!"

* * * * *

For a week before the operation that was to raise him from his servitude and inferiority to the level of a blind citizen, Nunez knew nothing of sleep, and all through the warm sunlit hours, while the others slumbered happily, he sat brooding or wandered aimlessly, trying to bring his mind to bear on his dilemma. He had given his answer, he had given his consent, and still he was not sure. And at last work-time was over, the sun rose in splendour over the golden crests, and his last day of vision began for him. He had a few minutes with Medina-saroté before she went apart to sleep.

"Tomorrow," he said, "I shall see no more."

"Dear heart!" she answered, and pressed his hands with all her strength.

"They will hurt you but little," she said; "and you are going through this pain—you are going through it, dear lover, for *me* . . . Dear, if a woman's heart and life can do it, I will repay you. My dearest one, my dearest with the tender voice, I will repay."

He was drenched in pity for himself and her.

He held her in his arms, and pressed his lips to hers, and

looked on her sweet face for the last time. "Good-bye!" he whispered at that dear sight, "good-bye!"

And then in silence he turned away from her.

She could hear his slow retreating footsteps, and something in the rhythm of them threw her into a passion of weeping.

He had fully meant to go to a lonely place where the meadows were beautiful with white narcissus, and there remain until the hour of his sacrifice should come, but as he went he lifted up his eyes and saw the morning, the morning like an angel in golden armour, marching down the steeps . . .

It seemed to him that before this splendour he, and this blind world in the valley, and his love, and all, were no more than a pit of sin.

He did not turn aside as he had meant to do, but went on, and passed through the wall of the circumference and out upon the rocks, and his eyes were always upon the sunlit ice and snow.

He saw their infinite beauty, and his imagination soared over them to the things beyond he was now to resign for ever.

He thought of that great free world he was parted from, the world that was his own, and he had a vision of those further slopes, distance beyond distance, with Bogota, a place of multitudinous stirring beauty, a glory by day, a luminous mystery by night, a place of palaces and fountains and statues and white houses, lying beautifully in the middle distance. He thought how for a day or so one might come down through passes, drawing ever nearer and nearer to its busy streets and ways. He thought of the river journey, day by day, from great Bogota to the still vaster world beyond, through towns and villages, forest and desert places, the rushing river day by day, until its banks receded and the big steamers came splashing by, and one had reached the sea—the limitless sea, with its thousand islands, its thousands of islands, and its ships seen dimly far away in their incessant journeyings round and about that greater world. And there, unpent by mountains, one saw the sky—the sky, not such a disc as one saw it here, but an arch of immeasurable blue, a deep of deeps in which the circling stars were floating . . .

His eyes scrutinised the great curtain of the mountains with a keener inquiry.

For example, if one went so, up that gully and to that chimney there, then one might come out high among those stunted pines that ran round in a sort of shelf and rose still higher and higher as it passed above the gorge. And then? That talus might be managed. Thence perhaps a climb might be found to take him up to the precipice that came below the snow; and if that chimney failed, then another farther to the east might serve his purpose better. And then? Then one would be out upon the amber-lit snow there, and half-way up to the crest of those beautiful desolations.

He glanced back at the village, then turned right round and regarded it steadfastly.

He thought of Medina-saroté, and she had become small and remote.

He turned again towards the mountain wall, down which the day had come to him.

Then very circumspectly he began to climb.

When sunset came he was no longer climbing, but he was far and high. He had been higher, but he was still very high. His clothes were torn, his limbs were blood-stained, he was bruised in many places, but he lay as if he were at his ease, and there was a smile on his face.

From where he rested the valley seemed as if it were in a pit and nearly a mile below. Already it was dim with haze and shadow, though the mountain summits around him were things of light and fire. The mountain summits around him were things of light and fire, and the little details of the rocks near at hand were drenched with subtle beauty—a vein of green mineral piercing the grey, the flash of crystal faces here and there, a minute, minutely-beautiful orange lichen close beside his face. There were deep mysterious shadows in the gorge, blue deepening into purple, and purple into a luminous darkness, and overhead was the illimitable vastness of the sky. But he heeded these things no longer, but lay quite inactive there, smiling as if he were satisfied merely to have escaped from the valley of the Blind in which he had thought to be King.

The glow of the sunset passed, and the night came, and still he lay peacefully contented under the cold clear stars.

www.ingramcontent.com/pod-product-compliance
Lightning Source LLC
Chambersburg PA
CBHW030414310726
48979CB00002B/411

* 9 7 8 1 6 2 7 3 0 1 2 8 2 *